The
MONK *of*
LANTAU

The MONK of LANTAU

MANN MATHARU

authorHOUSE

AuthorHouse™ UK
1663 Liberty Drive
Bloomington, IN 47403 USA
www.authorhouse.co.uk
Phone: 0800.197.4150

Published by AuthorHouse 31/07/2015

ISBN: 978-1-5049-8761-5 (sc)
ISBN: 978-1-5049-8762-2 (e)

Print information available on the last page.

Any people depicted in stock imagery provided by Thinkstock are models,
and such images are being used for illustrative purposes only.
Certain stock imagery © Thinkstock.

This book is printed on acid-free paper.

Because of the dynamic nature of the Internet, any web addresses or
links contained in this book may have changed since publication and
may no longer be valid. The views expressed in this work are solely those
of the author and do not necessarily reflect the views of the publisher,
and the publisher hereby disclaims any responsibility for them.

For you.

Acknowledgements

This story has been in my heart, mind, and soul since 2004, and it has stayed there for over eleven years. During that time there have been several people who have inspired me to write it. My close friends and loved ones, you know who you are, and you're in my heart always. I must say a special thanks to Monica LaSarre, my editor and close friend. Her contribution to this story has made it what it is. She has captured my imagination and helped turn the little words I had into readable piece of art, which I hope you all enjoy and share.

Contents

Prologue

The wisdom of enlightenment is inherent in every one of us. It is because of the delusion under which our mind works that we fail to realise it ourselves, and that we have to seek the advice and the guidance of enlightened ones.

—Hui-Neng

With the sun, the man arose from his tent, tidied his meagre belongings, and aimed his tired and bruised feet east. Surely he must be close now. Stopping only briefly for meditation during those times when his course seemed foggy and his heart clouded, he made steady progress.

How many days had he walked? He didn't know. The length of the journey, defining its extent by the measurements of mankind, seemed futile. They say journeys of the greatest importance tend to be that way – studded with an eternal beauty that dissipates when we try to mark it, map it, and chart it. No, the length and number of days he'd been travelling weren't as important as the steps he took to reach his goal. For with each step he took in the correct direction, his mind cleared and the Truth resonated deeply in his core, echoing in unison with the beat of his heart.

Regardless of how long it took for him to reach the location he sought and the blessed earth on which he would place the small figurine, it would be less painful to bind his own hand to a hot copper kettle than it would be to step away from the path he felt compelled to take. He'd known his entire life this journey would happen, and as the years passed, the compelling and pulsing pull of the tiny Buddha figurine refused to abate. Now, as an old man who would be better suited to aging gracefully under a grove of plum trees, he had finally embarked. So, no, it mattered not how long the journey took, because there was nothing left for him on any path diverging from this one true course.

In time, the weary traveller reached his destination and with a heart that unfettered itself of age with each step, he made his final ascent to behold the place. Trees as dark and stately as the oldest soul created an achingly pristine backdrop to the rise of the hill on which he placed the Buddha. The bronze figurine was small, small enough that he'd carried it in his pocket these many days of journeying and throughout the entirety of his adult life. He placed it with supreme care on a rock outcropping, light catching the bronze and awakening his senses with its otherworldly light. It belonged here. Though he could not have pictured the place before arriving at it, somewhere deep within he'd always known it would be this place, as certainly as he knew his hand from his foot. It had been an old knowledge, the type of wisdom we carry inside though we know not from where we obtained it.

He took a step backwards to behold the Buddha, who, in seated pose, had raised his right hand as a signal of removing affliction and laid his left hand in his lap in a gesture of giving *dhana*. The man kneeled at the Buddha's feet, hands clasped in front of his breast in reverent offering of *namaste*. His life had been spent healing others, sacrificing his own physical desires, and foregoing creature comforts to offer compassion and rest to those in need. As he knelt before the Buddha, at eye level with the lotus flower throne on which the Buddha sat, he felt cherished, watered, nurtured, and, in a way, rewarded for the myriad of gifts he'd given others. This was his reward, this moment of perfect peace, the end of his journey.

In that mysterious way in which the universe arranges things, however, this man, this healer, was not at the end of his journey. Rather, the true mark of his spiritual passage through this physical world was about to be made, etched and moulded into something eternal and lasting. The man stayed by the Buddha for three days and three nights, deep in meditation and prayer, in perfect symmetry and alignment with his life's purpose. Then, on the third day, he rose and walked into the thicket of trees that blanketed, protected, and cradled the small Buddha. There, with the most rudimentary of tools, he crafted a small hut with a thatched roof of stripped branches, braiding and weaving them into a simple covering from the elements. Having completed his shelter, he entered the hut and sat and waited.

The year was 1882. Since that time, word of the healer's gifts for curing, comforting, blessing, appeasing, and assuaging the pains of life had traversed the globe. Sometimes, for the right person on a journey of the purest of intentions, the enlightenment of the healer of Lantau has been found.

One

The Rain

Don't look to others to find yourself.

—Mann Matharu

Elle

I will never forget that day or the way it felt to be so alone, so utterly alone. In a city full of millions of people, who could possibly feel like the last standing person on earth? Yet I might as well have been. If London's drip-drip-dripping rain had ever for once just *stopped*, I might've been able to get a handle on my thoughts and rationalize a way out of this one. But that would've been asking too much, I guess.

The dripping was like a metronome, collecting tears from the sky in the pot I'd placed inside the front door, right under the leaky roof of our flat. Drip. Drip. Drip. Drip. Today of all days, with so much collecting in my mind, such a myriad of thoughts I needed to sort through, London's rain seemed like something worse than Chinese water torture.

"If I confess to knowing the identity of Jack the Ripper, will you just. Make. The rain. STOP!" I yelled at the ceiling, to nobody in particular, but hoping against all hope "somebody up there" would hear me and grant a miracle for a dry, sunny day.

I leaned back on the sofa that was worn with the years and curved in all the right spots, such that it cocooned me in aged, maroon velvet like a mum's hug.

Mum. She'd be home soon.

I threw off the quilt I'd been snuggling under and raced to the kitchen to boil some water for tea. A peace offering, perhaps? Guiltily, I got out the nice teacups, the ones we saved for guests, and a tin of her favourite lemon biscuits.

We'd been fighting for days. Weeks. Forever, it felt like. Maybe tonight, maybe this time when she came home, we could sit quietly together and have our tea and ignore the rain and find some commonality again.

"Bloody hell!" The shout from the foyer was audible, but tempered. Then there was the sound of a metal pan being kicked about.

My hopes for a quiet chat and some resolution to our differences dissipated like the steam from our teacups. Mum and the dripping water pan had collided, and now, thanks to the London rain, we were pacing towards another row.

"Elle, you could've warned me to watch out for that pan! A note on the door, something! Or were you too busy packing?" Mum's voice was dripping with displeasure.

She knew I'd be home, packing for Stockholm and my new life, and she could hardly stand it.

"No, Mum, I wasn't packing. I've decided to stay here, with you, and be an old maid working in a men's clothing shop and volunteering at an orphanage on weekends." My voice matched hers in sarcasm and disdain.

All was quiet then.

I heard her set down her things, hang up her coat, and walk softly to the kitchen. That was my mum: always orderly, always routine, always quiet.

"Really? You're … staying?" Her voice was soft, her face even softer. Though I could see the lines of worry around her eyes, she was still a young-looking woman for 50.

"No, Mum. I'm sorry; it was a poor excuse for humour. I'm still going." I felt terrible for having given her false hope. When would I ever grow up and stop hurting people? My whole life I'd felt I was doing everything wrong, like a cursed fool who was the butt of some cosmic joke, always hurting others, never able to find the right words to appease another's pain and give comfort. It was precisely why I had to go. I couldn't stay here alienating my friends and disappointing my mum any longer.

Sitting across from her at the small kitchen table, I started again.

"We've been over this, like, a gazillion times, Mum. You know this is my best chance. I missed so much school on bed rest that my grades suffered. University is not an option for me. I can't support myself on a low-wage job at the shopping centre forever, and, quite honestly, I don't want to. I have to go to Stockholm. This opportunity won't be open to me forever. Clerking as a legal intern is my wedge, my foot in the door to a legal career, earning a wage I can live on! You can't support me forever. You know you can't."

"The whole universe is in a glass of wine," came her reply, quietly.

"What? Wine? What are you talking about?" I asked.

She smiled then. It was the first I'd seen of her smile in longer than I cared to remember.

"Oh, it's a line from a poem. Your father and I ... we used to laugh about that line sometimes. His sister was a lawyer and mine was a poet, and holidays with those two together were miserable. Your father, he used to say poets and lawyers have only one thing in common."

"And what's that?" I asked.

"The words they use are not meant to be understood."

We were laughing then, together. I didn't often hear stories from her of my father, so it was special when she chose to share one from time to time.

"Elle, I just want so much more for you. A legal career will pay your bills, but it can be a self-serving industry and I just ... Well, I just *feel* like you were meant for more than that. You are here for something bigger than clerking in high heels every day for a bunch of suits talking legal jargon that makes no sense to anyone but themselves. Do you really think that will make you ... *happy*?"

I sighed. We'd had this same argument so many times. She just didn't understand what it was like to be twenty-two. Twenty-two and single. Twenty-two and single with no job. Twenty-two and single with no job and no job prospects and no income and no means to explore the world and have experiences and meet with your friends at the pub and actually be able to afford to buy a round of drinks. I knew those reasons for taking this internship sounded frivolous to her and shallow. But come on! Life was meant to be lived, and you had to have some money in your pocket to live it! My friends had moved on, had careers and were starting families. I had my mum, who was constantly trying to get me to "do something *big*" with my life, a leaky flat in London, no money to do anything with, and disillusionment with the sentiment that life was supposed to be my oyster at this age. Alone. I was alone.

"Mum, I'm ready to start my life, and getting involved in a career path that can help *fund* my life is what I need to do right now. I'm sorry. I know you're disappointed. I never wanted to hurt you."

I laid my hand on hers, squeezed it gently, and then quietly left the room to finish packing.

Zoe

I will never forget that day or the way it felt to be so alone, so utterly alone. I let myself into our flat after a long workday, and the solitude hit me like a wall of steel. No kicked-off sneakers on the foyer floor. No cereal bowls or teacups in the sink needing to be washed and put away. No bumping-thumping noise from the stereo in the bedroom, indicating Elle was home. Just the drip, drip, drip of the rain. Always there was the rain this time of year.

I turned on some soft music and sat on the velvet sofa that still had a lingering scent of Elle's perfume – jasmine and vanilla. The drops of rain hitting the pan on the floor of the kitchen, under the leaky roof, sounded like a metronome and lulled me into a sort of meditative peace. My mind started travelling and uncoiling. I embraced the aloneness and let my thoughts drift. Thoughts fleeted in and out, snagging other thoughts and floating like feathers through my sea of consciousness.

Elle. Stockholm. She won't be happy there. She was meant for more. More what? Dripping rain. It was raining the day she was born. Perhaps she was meant for a life of grief. Wish I could give her rainbows. She has to find the rainbows herself. I can't grasp them for her. Her dad would've known what to do. Ten years without him. Miss him. Miss him so much. Dripping rain. Elle. Did she make it to Stockholm? So much trouble with flights these days. Will she call? Should I call her? He would've known what to do. He gave her all he could give.

I must've slept for hours. When I awoke, by some miracle, the sun was shining through the windows. Saturday morning. That meant laundry and a trip to the market and watering the plants and sweeping the floors. The restorative sleep had worked its magic. I felt kissed by the sun. Despite all the chores I had ahead of me for the day, I knew exactly what I needed to do about Elle.

It was time. She needed to know the truth.

Matthew

I will never forget that day or the way it felt to be so alone, so utterly alone. My meeting at the office had gone long. They always went long these days. Merging our corporation with another had meant an endless parade of meetings and contracts and negotiations and decisions … Some days I just wanted to walk away from it all, head in no particular direction, feed the pigeons in the park, and let some breathing room from the office start taking the sharp edge off the perpetual pounding in my head.

But there was the family. They needed me. I wanted to give them so much. Holidays on the coast, a nicer home than we currently had in the suburbs, a car that was reliable, maybe even a dog. Or a cat. My daughter would love a cat.

My daughter.

Oh, sweet girl! I'm so sorry, I'm late again!

I shut the door of my office, then entered it once more, grabbed my briefcase, and shut it again, slamming it this time for emphasis. This office had made me late to pick up my princess, and I was determined to make somebody pay for it. The door was an unsuspecting victim.

I ran down the hall and out to the parking lot, jumped in the car, and wheeled my way into traffic. And that's when it started raining. Blast the rain! Always it was raining this time of year. The drip, drip, dripping of the raindrops pinging my windshield was making me cross. And there went the wiper blade. I knew I should've replaced that last weekend. Now I'd have a drive to the school in sheets of rain and rush hour traffic and *no wiper blade* to contend with. Couldn't a guy catch a break?

Doing my best to navigate the crowded streets, I kept a close eye on the time. She was let out of her after-school young artists program at five o'clock, too early for her mother to pick her up. Her mother didn't finish working until six. Of course, if I could ever catch a break and get that promotion I deserved, maybe her mother wouldn't have to work.

I didn't mind picking her up every day though, really. *She's a little chatterbox, always going on about rabbits she drew in art class and the apple juice she spilled in the lunchroom and "when can we go to the fair again, Daddy?"*

5.05 p.m.

Traffic jam now averted, I should be there in three minutes.

5.10 p.m.

Three minutes was optimistic. I should be there in five more minutes.

5.20 p.m.

Finally, there's the school.

I pulled into the parking lot and didn't see her. *She must be inside, staying out of the rain.* I walked through the driving sheets of water and entered the school. Still no brown-haired girl wearing pigtails. *Where could she be?*

I looked back through the glass of the school doors, out across the parking lot, and saw her standing next to the side of the road, with her little umbrella and her pink shoes sporting ribbons for laces, waving her artwork from today's watercolours class. She looked at me and smiled, waving her picture frantically.

Silly little girl. Knowing her, she probably thought she'd save me the time of having to park in the lot by just waiting for me by the road. Such a thoughtful girl.

I walked quickly from the school back to the car, yelling to my precious daughter through the driving rain, hoping she would hear.

"Honey, stay right there! I'll bring the car over! Try to stay dry under your umbrella, baby girl!"

I stooped to work the key into the door lock and was preparing to step inside the car when I heard it. *Brakes squealing. Screams. The crunch of an umbrella under something heavy … tires?*

Turning quickly, I saw her there. My daughter. On the road. There was so much blood. She was so still. And the car that had hit her was gone.

In that moment, my world stopped. Standing there in the blasted rain, I finally got the reprieve my throbbing head was craving after so many years of office meetings, deadlines, work, work, work. All of that dissipated in an instant, forgotten and so very far away. But it wasn't the reprieve I'd hoped it would be. In that moment, the rain was like a metronome, and the ping, ping, ping of water on the cold steel of cars lulled me into a stillness I never want to know again. Flashbacks of tying ribbons on shoes, going to get ice cream after dinner, holding the tiny hand of the most beautiful little creature love every created …

And then I came to and realised I was alone and looking at my baby girl lying on cold, wet concrete. Her watercolour lay next to her, smeared with mud, the colours running from being soaked in the rain. Never have I felt so alone. And the rain kept pouring down on us both.

Two

The Road Called Valour

Let the past be your guide, not your destination.

—Mann Matharu

Zoe

Sitting waterside in a café in the city centre of Stockholm was a blessing. To see Elle would be a blessing. To have been able to leave bustling London behind for a short weekend – even that was a blessing.

The breeze sweeping off of the Baltic Sea ruffled my hair. I watched the sails on the boats coming into the harbour – such magnificent colours and variety in those sails. *If I had a sailboat, I'd choose a lemon-yellow sail with green sprigs of grass in the forefront. It would be cheery and brighten my day. I'd sail the world and give myself space to stretch my mind with a pile of books beside me and the water lapping at the sides of my boat and no land in sight. Yes, a cheerful hermit, that's what I would be.*

"Your *kardamummabulle*, madam," said the voice at my elbow.

I looked up to see my waiter and secretly wished he hadn't ripped me so soon from my lovely daydream. One look at the buttery, golden pastry softened me though, and I smiled brightly in thanks.

"Another espresso, madam?" The waiter's voice was kind and he was eager to be of service. His smile was youthful, but his eyes looked older than his skin. *This young man has an old soul*, I thought.

"No, I don't think so. Perhaps some water would be good. I am waiting for someone and she is late. Another espresso maybe when she arrives," I replied.

"Of course. I'll bring the water to you, yes? I hope your guest, she is coming here soon, madam."

"Yes," I said. "I think she will arrive soon. She has an apartment close by and I can't imagine traffic would delay her. I think she would walk here."

"It is a busy day in the city. Many tourists make a quick walk through town very ... difficult. What does she look like, your guest? I can watch for her," he offered.

"Oh, she is my daughter, and people say we look alike. She's working in a legal office and probably will be wearing professional clothes. Brown hair, mid-length, sparkling blue eyes."

"She sounds very beautiful." He grinned mischievously. "My English, it is not so good, but I think I know this word *beautiful* very well. Beauty is universal word, I think. I will be sure to send her to you when she arrives at here."

I was wrong to come here. She should be here by now.

The lack of phone calls had been a surprise at first. The messages I'd left her were all unanswered, which became disturbing as the weeks wore on. A cryptic note from her here and there, to say she was all right and very busy, had grown offensive as weeks turned into months. My requests to visit or have her come to London were ignored. Finally, I'd done what any mother would have. I'd come to her. I had told her where I would be and when she could meet me, if she wished to. She had acknowledged receipt of the message with a short, non-committal "Okay," and nothing more.

A hundred sailboats must've drifted in and out of the harbour in the time I waited. I felt like I might just float away with them from all the water I'd had. The *kardamummabulle* long ago finished, it felt like I'd been sitting at this café table, itemizing my failures as a mother, for hours, rehashing my last conversations with Elle and desperately trying to pinpoint where our relationship had gone south. I was half a world away and lost in my own thoughts when the now-familiar voice of my waiter visited my ears again.

"Madam …" His voice was gentle. He pulled out the chair next to me and hesitated. "My shift, it is over. I can leave now, but I thought …"

His voice faded as I motioned for him to take a seat.

I looked at him, our eyes level for once, now that he wasn't standing above me to take my orders for more water, another espresso, a napkin for my tears.

"What is your name, young man?"

17

"I am Matteo," he said.

"And what do you do here in Stockholm, Matteo?" I probed gently, not wanting to pry, but grateful for someone to talk to after hours of waiting for Elle.

"Oh, well, I am an artist, actually. I work here in the coffee shop to earn money for art supplies and food, but art is my *paixão*. My passion." His eyes were caramel coloured, and they twinkled when he spoke of his art.

"You are not from here, I think." It was a statement, not a question.

"Right. I am not from here. I am from Brazil, actually. I moved here for a job that ... it did not work well for me. I loved the people and the boats," he said, motioning towards the harbour with a delicately boned hand. "And so I stayed. This place is where I belong."

"It must be lovely to practice your art as your occupation," I replied, truly meaning it. I thought of my job as an accountant for a pharmaceutical company, an entry-level position I'd managed to secure years ago, after ... It was so boring, so dull, so uninspiring.

"You also are not from here, I think," he said. Another statement.

"It's true. I am here from London, arrived just this morning, but it looks like I will be leaving soon. I guess I could even leave now." The tears welled up in my eyes.

We must've talked for hours, Matteo and I. Isn't it so beautiful when you meet a stranger and come to find yourself feeling such recognition, as if your souls have been kindred since before the beginning of time?

Leaving the café a short time later, we walked along the harbour, and our conversation ebbed and flowed and ricocheted off of green, yellow, and silver sails of boats. Our words were picked up and carried further into the depths of our souls, where we heard them, felt them, released them, and let the wind dive down and scoop them up and carry them along breezes destined for faraway shores.

Matteo said he felt he lived to share art with children. His studio was small and portable; all he needed was carried in a simple case he could strap on his back as he visited schools and shelters and street corners. Whenever and wherever he could, he set up his easel and lovingly took small hands in his and helped children release their feelings and emotions onto a page, brush in hand.

"They are such simple vessels, you know, with such honest and unjaded feelings to share. I never feel my time is a waste when a child gives me a glimpse into their world, through their eyes, of their feelings expressed on a canvas. It is so beautiful. It is a stunning gift they give me. In some small way, I hope that by giving them tools to express themselves, I am helping them cope with the world around them. Whatever their experience and circumstances, some of which I know are extremely sad – if they have an outlet, a blank canvas on which to express themselves, they will become healthy, feeling adults. One child and one canvas at a time, I hope I am able to make the world a more beautiful place," Matteo said. His broken English smoothed as he spoke of art, the words from his heart transcending the intricacies of our modern tongue like an age-old symphony of harmonious notes.

"I am so touched by the gift you give these children," I said. "I only wish my own daughter could see how precious our opportunities are to give of ourselves to help others."

"Your daughter is the beautiful girl who did not come to coffee, is that right?" he asked gently.

"Yes," I replied, not even attempting to hide my sadness at that point.

I told him then of Elle, of our last months together, of constant bickering and fights. I told him of my hopes for her and her dreams for herself, and then I shared her current plans for her time in Stockholm. He listened so patiently, with a wise silence that sounded the depths of my heart and delicately prompted me to discover in myself what hours of solitary thinking hadn't been able to uncover, without his ever saying a single word.

"I came here today to see her. I just wanted to see her, to know she is all right and to hold her in my arms. And I came to tell her a story. It was the story that brought me here, actually. I need to leave it with her, so she'll know it and so hopefully she'll let it affect her, her life and choices. It's her father's story, and she needs to hear it. And now, now I'll be leaving here with it instead. It doesn't belong with me anymore. It belongs here, in Stockholm."

"Zoe," he ventured quietly, and I realized it was the first time he'd used my name. "Zoe, would you share your story with me instead? At least then the story will be left in Stockholm, as you feel it should be."

A blast of cold air came from the harbour just then, and I looked up into the golden, scarlet, amber hues of the sun setting over the water.

We all have opportunities to share ourselves with others, I thought. *We just don't always get to pick and choose when we're called to share and with whom we're asked to share ourselves. The important thing is that we answer the call when it comes and not disregard it.*

Looking at Matteo, I resolved within myself that the story I'd come to Stockholm to share was meant to be shared here and now, though I grieved that it was not Elle's eyes that met mine.

That is how it happened that I began to recount a tale of a journey, of loss, and of recovery, a tale that changed my life and the lives of those closest to me forever.

I began …

Matthew

"I need to get to Hong Kong as quickly as possible," I said to the woman at the ticket counter. Judging by the number of hours I'd already been sitting and waiting and navigating traffic and other travellers, I thought I should at least be halfway to the moon by now, not standing at a ticket counter in Heathrow airport, only a scant sixteen miles from home.

"Sir, we have only one ticket left for a flight leaving tonight. We have several tickets for later in the week." The woman at the counter was all business, her hair pulled severely behind her head in a tight, no-nonsense bun.

"I'll take the one tonight, thank you."

"Brilliant! The total comes to £3,657. Will you be paying by card?"

"What? Are you sending me to the moon and back?" I had been sleep deprived, stressed to the max, and utterly spent for the past week, and the woman's smug recitation of the ticket price was the last straw.

"Sir," she said patiently, "last-minute tickets are always expensive, especially to go to a place as far away as Hong Kong. The only remaining ticket is also a first-class ticket. I'm sorry you're disappointed in the price. Would you like a less expensive ticket for next week instead?"

"I don't have until next week. By next week she could be dead already. I need to get to Hong Kong and back again to London in the next seventy-two hours or she will be lost to me!" I slammed my fist on the counter, and out of the corner of my eye I noticed the security guard look up and take a step closer.

"I'm sorry, sir. Maybe I could try …" Her fingers clicked away at the keyboard. "Give me just a moment, sir."

I waited. Impatiently. Shifting my weight from one foot to the next repeatedly, I drummed my fingers on the countertop, causing the woman to glance up in slight irritation, the first glimpse I'd had of her being anything but robotically professional since I'd stepped up to the counter.

"Ah!" She looked up at me and smiled. "I think I've found something for you."

My fingers stopped drumming and I held in my breath. "Yes, well, what is it?" I asked. I should have been *on* a plane by now, not still standing here negotiating which one to take!

"I can get you to Istanbul tonight …"

I didn't even let her finish before interrupting. *"Istanbul?* I'm trying to get to *Hong Kong*! Are you mad? Don't they teach you geography in that airport agent school of yours?"

The security guard took a step closer.

"Sir, I understand that you are trying to get to Hong Kong and not Istanbul and, despite what you must think, I *do* know that they are in fact not the same place, or even close neighbours of each other. What I was trying to say before being interrupted was, I can get you to Istanbul tonight and tomorrow afternoon I can get you on another flight to Hong Kong. We call them *connecting flights*, sir, and they are generally less expensive than—"

"Yes, yes, I'm not an idiot. I know what a connecting flight is!"

"Would you like a connecting flight to Istanbul then, sir?"

"How much?"

"Four hundred and forty five pounds."

"I'll take it," I said hastily and banged my fist again on the counter to seal the deal.

As I walked through security and to my gate, my blood pressure started to drop ever so slowly. The last week had been a whirlwind of activity and worry, and I felt like I was frizzing at the edges, like the hem of the tattered coat I was wearing that I was too cheap to replace. My wife was always trying to get me to buy a new one, but there were so many other bills to pay. Now we'd have a whole new set of them. Hospital bills, doctor bills, medicine bills, rehabilitation bills …

I thought of my sweet daughter, her small frame tucked under sterile white sheets smelling of bleach, the stark walls of her hospital room glowing with the red and green and blue lights of the instruments, machines, and monitors she was hooked up to. There had been an endless parade of doctors, nurses, specialists, chaplains, aides, and well-meaning, casserole-bearing neighbours and friends, all coming to offer condolences and assist in my little girl's care as well as they could.

I felt irritated by all of them. So many people, so much education and training in the brains of all those medical professionals we'd seen … so many second and third and fourth opinions. Not a single one of them could tell me something I wanted to hear. Not a single one of them could tell me that my sweet daughter would ever open her eyes and look at me and smile again.

The impact of the car had crushed her legs. They would heal, over time. The impact to her head as she hit the pavement had created massive haemorrhaging in her brain, and despite all their best efforts, Dr This and Dr That (I couldn't even remember their names any more) had informed me that "regrettably", my little princess was in an unstable coma, that she might or might not ever awaken from it. If she did awaken, which was unlikely, there would be damage.

In despair and racked with guilt (*Why had I been late to pick her up? Why couldn't I have just been on time for once?*), I'd raced from the hospital to the nearest pub and proceeded to get rip-roaring drunk for the first time in my life. Gone was the conservative, always responsible, conscientious employee, husband, and father. In his place was a sad, angry man with an open tab and a willing bartender.

Strangely, I didn't find myself face down in an alley come sunrise, as I understand can happen to those too inebriated to remember their names or addresses when the bar closes for the night. I don't know how it happened, I probably never will, but the fact remains: I'd found myself in a cab at 3 a.m., en route to my home and hopefully to my bed, and I'd poured out my guts, figuratively and literally, all over the back seat of the cab and to Rick, the taxi driver.

My tale of woe, my tale of being a responsible father and husband trying to do my best to seat my family well in life, my horrible propensity for being late to pick up my daughter, the accident, the hopelessness I felt as physician after physician had told my daughter's mother and I that she might not live, and my litre of whiskey – all came out in a slurred puddle of sobbing hopelessness.

Rick parked the taxi outside my house and turned around in his seat to face me.

"Listen carefully. Go inside, take a shower, sober up, pack your bag, and get yourself to Hong Kong. Once you're there, this is what you need to do …"

I didn't argue. I didn't ask for proof. I sat there in a pool of my own vomit and listened as this man I didn't even know gave me the biggest dose of hope I'd had in a lifetime. He told me of a way – the only way, he said – to help my daughter. And if I could help her, anything was possible.

An hour later, I'd written a note to my daughter's mum and left it on the kitchen counter, explaining where I'd gone and why, and was headed for the subway and Heathrow. More significantly, I'd set my toe on a road I'd never walked before. I turned and faced the road of the unknown, the untried, and the untested, the road whose only toll is that the traveller be despondent, worn down, desperate, and aching in the deepest part of his being for something he cannot seem to find. I stepped onto that road and never looked back.

Three

A Duality of Silence

*Be patient toward all that is unsolved in your heart and try
to love the questions themselves.
Do not now seek the answers, which cannot be given to
you because you would not be able to live them. And
the point is to live everything. Live the questions.*

—Rainer Maria Rilke

Matthew

Kimberly was the first boss I'd ever had who was a woman. A tall, leggy diva with golden tresses that fell over the shoulders of her neatly tailored pantsuits, Kimberly was my co-worker first, for years in fact, and then later my boss. The fact that we had both applied for the promotion, which she ultimately received, didn't seem to soften her towards me a single bit. We'd been adversarial as co-workers, each knowing the other was equally motivated towards upward mobility in the company, and as my boss you would've thought she might've given me some slack, since she obviously was the victor.

But no, *slack* wasn't a word in Kimberly's vocabulary. Where I'd been able to deal with her before as a fierce competitor, I could hardly stomach her now as my gloating, victorious boss who seemed hell-bent on letting the world know that she, a woman, had beaten out a man twice the experience with twice the education, and she was going to do what it took to make sure I didn't forget it.

That had been years ago. Reluctantly, I'd stayed in my same position, but not before pricing up salaries at other companies. My seniority with the company, though it hadn't included a promotion in fifteen years, at least was paying me a decent wage, one I couldn't have come close to if I had chosen to escape Kimberly and change companies.

When your family is counting on you for a pay cheque, you'll make a lot of sacrifices. Kimberly was my sacrifice, my Waterloo, the constant pit in my stomach.

What made me think of Kimberly just now? I tried to recall.

I stretched out my legs, or at least imagined I was stretching them, hoping against hope that an additional six inches of leg room had magically appeared under the seat in front of me since the last time I'd tried to stretch, about three minutes ago. *Airplane travel is for short people. Why didn't I take a train?*

Despite my having stood in front of the airline agent at the ticket desk for several agonizingly long minutes, I was severely annoyed with myself for not having bothered to notice her name. Her faux professionalism had been annoying, and I'd intended to complain to the airline at the first opportunity. Without a name, that was going to be difficult.

I'll just call her Kimberly, even if only to myself. It was a good, generic name for a classy lady who was standing in my way, which fit both my boss and the ticket agent perfectly.

Despite Kimberly's promise of a late afternoon flight to Istanbul, I'd ended up on a red-eye flight. The airline clerk at the gate had informed me that, "quite regrettably", they had oversold my flight, and since mine had been the last ticket sold, I automatically was bumped to the next flight. A glance at my watch had revealed the next flight was a scant seven hours away.

Utterly annoyed and starting to feel a bit light-headed from my boozing stunt last night, I'd walked the airport, trying to rid myself of some anxiety, and had downed an endless parade of bottles of water. Though significantly better hydrated, the water had sent me to the men's room more often than I usually would've tolerated in such a germ-infested place as a public airport. Too raw to digest anything, my stomach simply cowered within me, silently begging me to keep the whiskey away and avoid spicy, overly salted airport food.

It had been a long seven hours of pacing the terminal and staring into a sea of faces, faces who were as much strangers to me as my recollection of what it must feel like to be well rested and happy with your life. I thought a lot about my daughter during my walking, but all those thoughts just made me feel more tired, more helpless, more of a failure. *If I hadn't been working late, trying to keep the boss happy, I could've made it on time to pick her up ... and this never would've happened.*

Finally, when I could not have walked another loop around the terminal if my life had depended on it, a voice over the loudspeaker (too cheerful a voice for a midnight flight, in my opinion) informed the strangers and me that it was time to board our plane.

I had sunk wearily into my seat and closed my eyes only seconds before I was asked to stand up and let someone crawl over me to the window seat.

I bet Kimberly assigned me a middle seat on purpose. She knew how uncomfortable I'd be here, wrestling two strangers for my 3/8-inch section of our shared armrests. Somehow she thought I deserved it, I just know it. I should've taken a train. It would've been faster, at the rate this blasted airport moves people through. Why didn't I take a train?

I opened a magazine then, a grimy thing I'd found in the seatback pocket in front of me, and braced myself for some mind-numbingly dull reading and take-off from the tarmac. I opened the obnoxiously glossy publication to the middle somewhere. (Did it really matter where I started reading? The whole thing was bound to be boring as all hell anyway.) I kept muttering under my breath all the while, "A train would've been better," and was knocked out of my repetitive mantra by the words of an ad in the magazine. A sophisticated, sexy woman was opening a gorgeous gift from a dapper man hovering at her shoulder, smiling. The inlay showed a diamond-crusted wristwatch and the slogan, "Be careful what you wish for. You just might get it."

I shut the magazine quickly. Was it only coincidence that the very moment I'd repeated for a hundredth time my wish for a train, not a plane, I saw the words, "Be careful what you wish for"?

The plane was in flight now, and my two seatmates were snoring softly. Sitting still was going to be the hardest thing about this flight. I needed to walk again. I needed to see something new, something different, something other than the back side of the man's head in front of me for the next several hours. I needed to pace myself, not be paced by this plane and some big corporate airline.

Surely it had been a coincidence, hadn't it? I felt sure it was. After all, I wasn't one of "those people" who believed in signs and wonders and all manner of hocus-pocus about the universe guiding us. No, I was a religious man who diligently attended church, but that's where it ended. God was up there, maybe, and I knew I was certainly down here, but the middle ground of communication between us was some sketchy business I didn't subscribe to. My wife, on the other hand, had been praying dutifully for our daughter. I figured I would just leave her to it. I couldn't bring myself to pray to a God I wasn't sure even gave a damn about the sufferings here on earth.

I rested then, and for the first time in weeks, I dreamt.

In my dream I was explaining to my boss why I couldn't be at work, why my daughter was in the hospital, and why I had to leave her bedside to travel halfway around the world to Hong Kong.

"Rick told me about the monk, someone who can help me, Kimberly." I pleaded with her for time away from my desk for my journey.

"You'd better be back in a week or I'm giving your job away to someone who realizes how stupid it is to follow the crazy instructions of a London cab driver." Her tone was unforgiving, unrelenting, unwelcoming, just like in real life. "Why in the world would you think a cab driver could help your daughter by sending you on this wild goose chase? You're an idiot."

And then my wife was there too. Her underlying message held as much doubt as Kimberly's had, but somehow it was sadder, and definitely not as sharp-toned.

"Oh, Matthew, I found your note, and what am I supposed to tell our daughter when she asks for you? That you went on a vacation? You know she associates planes with fun holidays, right? How am I to explain you're on a quest for her healing? She won't understand, I'm sure. Besides, Matthew, there are several new doctors I wanted to call, a few new treatment options we haven't tried yet. Maybe you could just come home and we could try something more, you know, more traditional? And what were you doing in a cab in the middle of the night anyway?"

And then Rick was there, whom I'd never even met before last night. Rick, who had spoken words to me that seemed so foreign, yet rang with so much truth, like the vibrations of the pipe organ that tingled every cell in my body as I sat in the pews on Easter morning at St Barnabas. *Reverberate*, I think that's the word. His words reverberated truths I could recognize as truths but couldn't understand.

"Matthew, you know what to do when you get to Hong Kong, don't you? You remember the instructions I gave you, right? This trip will help you. You'll see. I promise. Find that monk and he will show you …"

Ice cubes jolted me out of my sleep and back into the crowded compartment of the plane. I looked down to see a soda spilled across my lap, ice cubes melting into my pants and an embarrassed flight attendant paused mid-reach, an outstretched arm holding an empty cup between the aisle where she stood and the window seat where my armrest-thieving seat companion sat.

"I am so sorry, sir. Here, let me get you a napkin." Her voice was mighty chipper for, oh, what was it now, three in the morning?

"Who drinks soda at three in the morning?" I asked grumpily.

"Again, sir, I am so very sorry. Here, please take this voucher. I'll happily serve you a cocktail of your choosing, to express my apology." The flight attendant was trying, I'd give her that. But my dream had been so good, and Rick had been telling me something. Now I'd probably not be able to get back to it.

"Who drinks cocktails at three in the morning? I am trying to sleep, for Christ's sake!" I exploded, with an edge in my voice that bordered on anger.

"Forgive me, sir," she said, and retreated.

I settled back into my seat, hogged the entire armrest on both sides, squared my shoulders – defiantly daring either of my neighbours to do something about it – and tried to get back to my dream.

It was gone, though. As hard as I tried, I couldn't make it back to that place where Rick's words were comforting me, encouraging me that my journey would end well. So I did the only reasonable thing a hard-working father and husband could do when he was a mile high in a crowded plane and flying farther and farther away from his hospitalized daughter: I pretended I was sleeping, while instead I agonized over my decision to take the directions of a cab driver. I replayed countless arguments my wife and I had had regarding our daughter's care, how we were going to pay for it, what we would do if she passed away, how we would live without her, and when I should try to get back to work before I risked losing my job.

The plane was so quiet. Most of the passengers had been lulled into sleep by the rocking of the aircraft through the dark night sky. Silence is a strange thing. It drives some to madness, it's a refuge for others, and still for some, it gives our minds time to think, to question, to wonder. As much as I was happy for a few hours of no one talking at me, no phones ringing, no strangers to look at, I hated how quickly my mind jumped to the conclusion that it was time to overpower me with doubt and endless questions about my intentions, my plans, my itinerary, my hopes for the journey, and on and on.

I departed the plane a few hours later and set foot in Turkey for the first time ever, much more exhausted than when I'd entered the plane. My sleep, though I'd been happy for it when it finally came, had not been restful; rather, it had been yet another opportunity to replay all my doubts and failures.

And yet, for some reason, I didn't have the gumption to complain, and I didn't curse under my breath, and I didn't wish for a train. Maybe I was simply too exhausted. I just stood there in the morning heat of a new day in Istanbul and soaked in the rays of sun, happy to be on the ground and en route to finding the monk. Yes, I was on a path and only one more plane ride away from Hong Kong. I hoped Kimberly had booked a better seat for me this time.

I had a strange inclination then, something hinging on regret. I glanced behind me, hoping to catch a glimpse of the flight attendant. For some odd reason, I felt the need to apologize. I had been short with the girl and I wished to explain myself, how tired and stressed I was. I'd been ugly to her and I wanted to make it right. But she was nowhere to be seen.

Four

Silence in Chaos

*Sitting quietly, doing nothing, Spring
comes, and the grass grows, by itself.*

—Matsuo Bash

Elle

Mum had come to Stockholm and left again, and I, well, I had been unable to face her. We needed this time, she and I, to create some separation between us. Now a full-grown adult, I had to train her to stop being the hovering, overly concerned mum she'd been all these years. She had to recognize that I was here to become the grown-up I needed to be, and that no amount of motherly attention, including spur-of-the-moment trips to see me, was going to change my course.

My internship at the law office was everything I'd hoped it would be. Not only was I learning the ropes quite easily, I was enjoying the camaraderie of new co-workers and celebrating court victories over pints in corner pubs after hours. I loved getting dressed for work every morning, putting on sleek pants and silky shirts with matching heels, seeing the reflection of a successful, self-sustained, capable young woman in the mirror. No one could take that from me now. I wouldn't let anyone muddy this path with emotional snags of longing, missing, and regretting, especially not my mum.

I'd see Mum at the end of the year, for Christmas perhaps, and that would have to be enough for her.

Matthew

"What exactly do you mean, there is no reservation?" My voice was tempered yet insistent, and I was quite impressed with myself for not having lost my temper. Yet.

"Sir, what I mean is, I see that you are here in Istanbul, and I see that there are no further reservations for you by any airline leaving this airport for the next thirty days," stated the calm man at the ticket counter. He apparently was not having to work as hard as I was to stay calm. He was simply a calm person. He probably didn't even lose his temper when he got a flat tire or spilled his coffee or worked overtime because his boss forced him to. He had no lines on his face, just the clear, wrinkle-less complexion of a man in his fifties, with a thick crown of dark, well-groomed hair and eyes the colour of mocha.

"I see," came my equally calm reply. Something about this man challenged me from behind the curtain of those long, black eyelashes and that cool demeanour. He wanted to see if I was going to lose my temper so he could show me how much stronger a man he was when he didn't lose his. Well, I could play that game too.

I swallowed the bile that rose from my stomach in automatic response to the negative thought that Kimberly had struck again, and this time, she had made the most egregious of errors. She had packed me off to Istanbul without a way onward to Hong Kong. Had it been miscommunication or malicious intent? I would never know.

"Thank you for this information. I am surprised by it, but will wait here patiently as you, if you could be so kind, look into some options for me. You see, I need to get to Hong Kong, please, and very, very soon." I even smiled as I said it.

"Ah, I see. Well ..." The man hesitated and then began clicking away at his keyboard. "It would appear," he said after a few moments, "your options are limited to a flight leaving in two weeks directly to Hong Kong, or to a train departing tomorrow afternoon that will take you to Tehran, Iran, and include a flight directly upon arrival to Ulaanbaatar, Mongolia. You would need to find your own transportation after that to Hong Kong, but I think flights are fairly frequent and available."

I gritted my teeth, hopefully imperceptibly, and then smiled with as much gusto as I could, as if this man had just told me the greatest news of my life.

"Oh, a train, that's brilliant! I have always loved a train ride. Yes, certainly, please book me on the train. Thank you!"

Be careful what you wish for. You just might get it. A flashback to the magazine ad fleeted before my eyes, and I caught my breath. *It was no coincidence.*

The man was watching me closely, obviously waiting for the explosion he'd anticipated from me, as if I had a stamp on my forehead that had forewarned him somehow that "contents are under pressure; handle with care!"

He then he bowed his head, clicked away at his keyboard, asked for my payment, and handed me a ticket.

"Might I suggest taking in the sights of our stunning city while you wait for your train? Istanbul is a rare jewel, and it is few who have the opportunity to see it on a day as fine as this one is." The man handed me a stack of pamphlets and brochures and wished me a good day, smiling graciously.

Ten minutes later, I was in the back of a cab, being whisked through Istanbul en route to the coastal side of the country, along the Sea of Marmara. I was caught between berating myself for allowing that infernal man to force me into complying with his less-than-ideal solution of waiting a day for a train, and enjoying the strange calmness that had come over me. *I have no time to waste with sightseeing. Perhaps if I'd been more insistent, I could be on a flight by now. On the other hand, I was simply too tired to argue. It might give me sustenance for the road ahead if I take some time to walk a bit and get a solid meal and a good night's rest.*

While the cab driver darted in and out of city traffic, demonstrating all the skills of an adept autobahn driver, I leaned back in my seat and quietly looked out the window. I could fudge my way through enough French and German to make light conversation with most cab drivers throughout Europe, but here in Turkey, I was forced into silence by my lack of any knowledge whatsoever of the native tongue. I had smiled at the cab driver and pointed my finger instructively at the pamphlet I held; he'd nodded his acknowledgement, and that was the end of our conversation. Now, in silence, I sat alone with my thoughts.

I thought of my daughter, of course, and wondered if there had been any change in her condition. I thought of my wife, knowing she surely had found my note by now, and wondered how she was faring without me there. Thoughts snaked between my daughter, my wife, my job – my present, future, and past.

I thought most about my past and my daughter. I remembered when she first learned to ride her bike. My wife and I had held our breaths as she wobbled and weaved down the sidewalk in front of our home, riding for the first time without training wheels. Of course, she had fallen and scraped her knee, and her mum and I had raced to her side to comfort her. With those little arms wrapped around my neck and her tears dampening my shoulder, she'd exclaimed that she would never, ever ride again.

"My darling, you *must* try again. Every time you fall, you must pick yourself up and try again," I'd said to her. "Sit calmly on your bike, take deep breaths, and focus on your destination. You might fall, you might not; you might go fast, you might go slow; but regardless, every time you try again, you are getting one step closer to being a big girl who rides a bike."

It's so easy to dole out advice to others, isn't it? How often the advice we've given others fails to show itself when we ourselves are in the same situations that warrant it.

I might fall, I might go fast, and it sure seems like I might end up going slow … but I have to keep going, too.

I had worked for so many years with so few holidays and even fewer opportunities to travel and see the world. And here I was, whether I wanted to be here or not, in Turkey, a cradle of ancient civilization. How foolish I would be to miss a chance to see a bit of the grand city of Istanbul.

When the cab driver left me at a street corner a few moments later, it was with a renewed mindset that I set foot on the cobbled street and emerged into the sunlight. Having given myself permission to sightsee and enjoy it as best I could, I breathed deeply and looked around. My eyes lifted to the skyline, and in the distance I saw the spherical dome of the Hagia Sophia, surrounded by the solid masonry of her four corner towers. I directed my steps towards the ancient sanctuary, determined to reach it by foot and take in the sights of the crowded streets on my way. I had the time and found myself relaxing into the luxurious warmth of this fact.

The pamphlet, blessedly written in English, had educated me on the timeless treasure that is the Hagia Sophia. Constructed in AD 537, the stunningly beautiful landmark was the site of a Greek Orthodox basilica, a Catholic cathedral, an imperial mosque, and now a museum. What I found most fascinating was that, regardless of the religion laying claim to it as a sanctuary over the years, the same descriptions of reverence were voiced by all people: *Shrine of the Holy Wisdom of God* and *Place of Holy Peace*. To be so close to a location acclaimed worldwide as a sanctified edifice, with such a long history of being a focal point for a variety of religions with their own names for God and their own ways of worship, I knew I couldn't miss a chance to see this sanctuary for myself.

Melancholy came over me as I walked. I found it hard to be in a hurry in this place. In Istanbul, the past stubbornly clings to the present and persists in the cut stone of the streets and the faded glory of storefronts. Men walked arm in arm, displaying a common sign of friendship and peace; women in dark clothing passed by me, staring openly at my other-worldly appearance with curiosity, though not unkindly. I stared back, as I might have looked at the close-up faces of exotic animals in a menagerie, noticing intricacies and details, which transformed the faceless inhabitants of this old city into people, just like me. A nod here, a smile there, I found myself communicating without words to those around me, those who were drawn for a multitude of reasons to this same block of this same city on this same day, to share in experiencing what this moment in Istanbul had for us. I have never felt so much a part of a group as I felt, quite strangely, in this city filled with people I couldn't speak to, couldn't ask questions of – people with whom I could only share a patch of sunlight and a breath of fresh air.

It was the scent of Istanbul that caught me off guard the most. Gone was the damp smell of rain soaking through discarded newspapers and dripping off of bricks coated with lime and moss that I was accustomed to in London. Here, the air was a veritable carnival of aromas that confused my senses and piqued my curiosity. Spices danced on the breeze, teasing me with questions of their origin, daring me to investigate this shop and that, challenging me to name them and remember them and savour them. People passing by me left the lingering, musky scent of their bodies, warm from the sun, not the overpowering mix of perfumes and cologne that made me sneeze in the business district I was accustomed to walking through back home.

A busy day in the merchant district though it was, the chaos of shoppers and onlookers and tourists taking it all in was anything but overwhelming. The barking of merchants across the alleyways, calling to those in the street to come to their shops; the laughing of barefoot children chasing each other through the streets; and the clucking of women as they examined trays overflowing with produce ricocheted off the stone walls of buildings and houses. I felt as though I were hearing an orchestra and their ode to humanity, to life, to being present. It was not chaos; no, it was music to my ears.

As I reached the Hagia Sophia, the disparity between the noise of the merchants behind me and the cool click of heels on the marble as I climbed the steps of the sanctuary made for an interesting dichotomy. The noise of the one was bustling and boisterous; the other was just as alive, but a hallowed sound, something sanctified and reverent. From the moment I read the history of the Hagia Sophia in the cab earlier that morning, I had wanted to see and experience this place for myself. Once inside, I held my breath and realised the elaborate exterior encased a far superior and surpassingly magical interior, where I could scarcely believe I was seeing such abundant opulence. It wasn't just the architecture that drew my interest, nor the art of prayer rugs and mosaics, though both were compelling and stunning. I had always wanted to know what it would be like to sit in a place like this, where for centuries the masses of people long past had found solace and comfort in religious worship and the traditions of their spirituality. Truly, if there was a magical place on earth, this was it.

I have never considered myself a spiritual person, yet the draw to have a spiritual experience – something undeniably bigger than my mental capacity could explain away – had always been there, silently lurking. *Maybe someday,* I had thought, *if I could have a really phenomenal spiritual experience, something powerful and mystical, I could believe in something bigger than what my eyes see. I could pray like my wife does, and walk a spiritual path like I know others do.*

I entered the sanctuary and walked its corridors, admiring the colours and lights and feeling of this place. Here, it was different than in the crowded streets. No one took notice of me. No one nodded or smiled or even stared. Everyone was quietly, unobtrusively focused elsewhere. While their eyes appeared to be glancing upward or sideways at the displays along the walls, it wasn't really where their eyes were looking. Everyone here seemed to be focused inward, as if they, like me, were full of expectation and checking frequently to see if they were feeling *something* yet, something they came here expecting to feel. And I couldn't say whether anyone felt anything or didn't. I know I sure didn't. For all its beauty, the Hagia Sophia held nothing more for me than that of any of the astounding museums I'd visited in London or Paris.

Puzzled, I sat down on a wooden bench to rest my feet. My expectations for having a spiritual experience in this place had been high, I realised. With a sigh, I resigned myself to the fact that this was, perhaps, just another in a long line of tourist attractions the world held open for us to see. Yes, it was beautiful; yes, it was stunning; yes, it was old. But it was just walls and adornment and marble and remnants of days long past. And yet I was deeply saddened by my disappointment that there wasn't more for me here.

Glancing up, my eye was caught by the slow, graceful movement of a small family making their way through the crowds. I couldn't say what it was about them that drew my attention. They weren't dressed in remarkable style or unusual in their appearance in any way. They were just a normal-looking family: a father wearing dark slacks and a baggy coat draped over his slight frame, a small-boned woman with greying hair flowing down her back, and a small child between them grasping their hands. The child's face was streaked with tears that cut a swath through dirt-stained skin to reveal a peachy complexion underneath.

Why the tears? I wondered.

I studied them as if they were the most fascinating creatures I'd ever seen. They made their way through the crowd to the front of the sanctuary, up the steps to the altar, to a landing where hundreds of candles had been lit.

After digging in his pocket, the man handed a coin to an altar boy waiting in stillness to the side. The man gave a candle to the small child. She grasped it in her tiny hands and patiently waited while the boy stepped forward to light it for her. She closed her eyes and stayed there for several long moments, head bowed, candle illuminating her pensive face. Opening her eyes, glancing first at the man and then at the woman, she took a few steps forward and set her candle on the altar alongside the others. Just as quietly, just as gingerly, the man, woman, and child retreated down the steps, across the room, and out the main doors to the bustling streets below.

I realised I'd been holding my breath, and found relief in finally exhaling. Why had their few, modest actions captured my attention and kept me so deeply enthralled?

I decided to retrace their steps, walk their same path, and attempt to understand what it was they had experienced. Moving from my wooden bench, I slowly walked through the crowds, appreciating the silence and hushed tones and echoes bouncing off the domed ceiling above me. As they had done, I fished in my pocket for a coin for the altar boy, waited while he lit the candle, and then held it just below my chin. I closed my eyes. I stood quietly. It felt good to hold the warmth of the candle and feel the stillness around me.

I don't know how long I stood there. It must have been longer than a few minutes because I felt a bit of wax slide down the candle and give me a sharp twinge of pain as its heat hit the skin of my hand. And yet I didn't wince from the pain, I acknowledged its presence only. When I was ready to, I opened my eyes. It was if I were reborn and opening them for the very first time in a new world. Colours were bright around me. I felt an energy in my presence that was equal parts comforting, enlivening, and motivating. I felt I needed to do something, but was also content simply to stay where I stood. I felt light as a feather, though my fingers tingled with a sensation much weightier. I felt alive. I felt different.

I felt reborn. I didn't wipe away the tears that fell from my eyes. I embraced them, owned them, loved them, and allowed my heart to overflow with the gratitude, peace, and comfort they brought.

It was only as I made my way back to the streets of shouting merchants and noisy children that I realised what the magic of the Hagia Sophia really was. It certainly wasn't the magic I was hoping for, but undeniably magical just the same. In that place, for once, with nowhere to be and nowhere to go, I had allowed myself to be taken over by the silence around me. No ringing phones, no yelling boss, no honking horns … No, it had just been me, the whisper of a flickering candle, the beating of my heart, and a blessed silence that had taken me far away from the bustling world for a few magical moments. I had opened my eyes and felt more in tune with my surroundings than I had ever felt before. The Hagia Sophia drew me into an inescapable silence, and that magical silence rested me and refreshed me.

I wondered as I walked if such a silence was only attainable in that place, or if somehow, in the chaos of my life and the world around me, I could locate it once more without being in Istanbul. I hoped quite desperately I would be able to find it again.

Five

A Discovery of Strength

Forgiveness is a sign of strength, not weakness.

—Mann Matharu

Elle

I came home late from work to my rented flat. Swinging open the door and kicking off my shoes, I prepared myself for the rush of relief I usually felt upon coming home. After a hectic day at the law firm, with deadlines looming and constant chatter, I'd come to relish the solace of my private living area. I rarely turned on music, preferring the peace and quiet of perfect solitude as a balance to the day's pace.

A slip of paper was on the floor right inside the door, a bright orange note that had been tucked underneath. I picked it up and saw that it was from my neighbour, indicating a package had been delivered to me earlier in the day. *Who would be sending me a package?*

I knocked on the neighbour's door and, after a quick exchange of pleasantries, returned home, large box in hand. The return address indicated it was from my mum, the first tangible piece of anything from her since I'd moved.

Holding my breath, I quickly ripped open the cardboard to reveal the contents and exhaled when I saw what it contained.

Art supplies? New charcoals and paper? Brushes and acrylic paints?

I had purposely left behind all of my art supplies in London, thinking I wouldn't need them or have time for them in my new life. But Mum knew me well, as much as I hated to admit it.

I sat down with a fresh page and inhaled the intoxicating scent of the new tray of charcoals. I think I sketched for hours, but couldn't be sure exactly how long it was. By the time I leaned back to survey my creation, the sky was dark and the moon had risen high. I was breathing so softly, so contentedly, inhaling my mum's precious gift and exhaling the stress of my new career. For a brief moment, my flat seemed wretchedly quiet and lonely. I would've loved to have Mum there to snuggle up with next to a tray of tea, and I started to cry. In truth, I felt pangs of regret at having missed the chance to see her when she came to Stockholm. Hovering parent or not, I missed her.

Matteo

Zoe's story was disarming me completely. Sitting next to the harbour and this kind, lovely, and compassionate woman, there was no place I would rather have been. Though the day was growing late and I had plenty of things to attend to, I only knew that I wasn't prepared yet to leave the fireside of the glowing embers of Zoe's story. So I cuddled up next to them in my heart and listened.

Sometimes we come to chasms in our lives and find ourselves looking far across to the other side. Just as we begin to wonder how we will make it across, a helper comes along. Before we know it, in a matter of minutes, in the time it takes to share a hug or hear a story, we have crossed over and are looking back at the shell of who we were when we first approached the chasm. Now I also had crossed over and was staring back with only slight recognition at the man I'd been that morning, even as I settled comfortably into the skin of the man I had become by day's end. Just like that. It happened so quickly.

What was it about her story that had shuffled me?

It was not so much the details, the concrete facts, and the relaying of events that had disarmed me. Rather, her story watered me by the feeling and underlying message of it. I had opened myself to the unspoken wisdom hidden deep within her tale, and as I did, I felt the influx of waves of delight, inspiration, and hope flowing into me. I needed to let those same waves flow out to whatever destination they were intended for. After all, it is said that to whom much is given, much is required. And through Zoe's story, I was given so much, too much to keep to myself. So I continued listening, contemplating the magic of the day's events and enjoying the overflow of gratitude for all I was being taught on this day.

Matthew

Bloody hell. The train was late, of course.

When it finally did arrive and I boarded, I sank with relief into the cushion of my seat. Utterly spent physically from yesterday's walking through the markets and streets of Istanbul; tapped emotionally from my exercise of patience with the calm man at the airport and the incompetent housekeeper last night, who couldn't seem to get the hot water working in my rented room; the only part of me that felt rested was, strangely, my soul. The Hagia Sophia had been good for me, I surmised.

I had even rested well on the hard-as-nails bed in the bed and breakfast last night and arisen early to the sound of morning prayers at daybreak. The east-facing calls of the devout were undeniably exuberant and foreign, but not annoyingly so. Sipping quietly on the exquisite bitterness of Turkish coffee, brought to my room by the decidedly more competent daytime housekeeping staff, I had closed my eyes and envisioned myself once again in the sanctuary of the Hagia Sophia, experimentally trying to arrive back at that place of rejuvenating solidarity. I found it easily once again, to the sound of prayers of strangers in a foreign land.

As the train jolted into motion and began its trek down the tracks, I sat quietly in my seat. I had an entire three-seated row to myself and normally would have congratulated myself on the good luck. Instead, I found myself longing for someone to talk to, someone to share my new experience with. Looking around me at the faces of travellers in our shared train car, I realised I really ought to congratulate myself after all: in the packed train, I was the only one with a row to myself. Feeling somewhat luckier than normal, I settled into my small area and closed my eyes for a short nap. The express train would've taken me to Tehran within twenty-four hours, but there wasn't an express train running until next week. The next train to Tehran would take just under three days because of the multiple stop-overs, and though I'd picked up some books to read along the journey, somehow a nap seemed a more suitable option.

I hadn't been dozing long when I heard the voice of a woman at my shoulder. Speaking directly into my ear, she said, "*Affedersiniz, efendim!*"

"Wait, what? What's that?" I opened my eyes groggily and with a fair amount of alarm.

"*Lütfen, efendim …*" The train attendant was shaking my shoulder and pointing frantically at the aisle behind her.

"I'm sorry, I don't speak Turkish …" I stammered, gesturing as best I could with my hands in some ignorant form of sign language.

"Oh, I see … It is not a problem, Sir. I speak your English."

I started to get annoyed then, wondering whether or not waking up passengers was a one-day or two-day lesson taught in flight attendant and train attendant schools. They all seemed to do it really well, regardless of what mode of transportation I chose!

Remembering then how regrettably ugly I had been to the flight attendant on the route from London, I thought better of my knee-jerk reaction, which would've included a raised voice and probably another sign language symbol that was universally understood.

Instead, I sighed and cheerfully asked what I could do to help the woman.

"There is a passenger, sir, he is very … how do you say it? He is very … sick, ill! Please, he needs to lie in your seat. For rest! You will move to other seat, okay?" She smiled and gestured with her hands for me to follow.

One look at the green-looking man waiting to lie down in my row of empty seats was all it took. I obediently followed the attendant to a new seat, amazed at my own acquiescence. The seat to which I was led was a window seat, and I crawled over a sleeping man and a woman knitting a red cap in order to reach my tiny destination. Just as I sat, I heard retching coming from the seat I had vacated moments ago, and apparently just in time.

Resigned to my fate of riding for days in squished silence, I closed my eyes and thought of my daughter and recalled how much all of this was worth it if I could just get back to her in time.

The day passed without incident. The following day, still on the train, an announcement was made that we would soon be stopping to refuel and allow new passengers on. Within moments, we had pulled into a train station in the midst of a brown field, which I was told was somewhere west of the Iranian border.

With an hour of layover time, I extracted myself from the cramped seat and stretched my legs, taking the opportunity to walk outdoors and breathe deeply of fresh air. A dirt road ran alongside the tracks, and as long as I didn't stray too far, I felt comfortable enough in this strange and often dangerous part of the world to walk down it for a few minutes. The miles of nothingness, of barren brown earth, spanned endlessly on both sides of the road. So imagine my surprise when I walked over a rise and saw a group of men surrounding a large firepit.

Their dress was drab and earth-toned like the landscape. I stopped to watch them. They stopped their activities to glance briefly at me. Though I lingered to watch them, they seemed to know I didn't pose a threat and returned to their labour, what appeared to be an all-too-modern chore in this all-too-ancient part of the world: burning trash.

The flames leaped and consumed paper and cans and packages and other rubbish. From each of the ten men's satchels, worn tied to their backs but now hanging low in front of them, handfuls of rubbish were methodically placed on the burn. Over and over and over again, they reached into their packs, placed rubbish on the fire, and then reached in again. Once emptied, their satchels were very evidently lighter. The men, having extinguished the burn, turned to walk away, laughing and jostling each other light-heartedly.

As I walked back to the train station, I wondered how long they'd travelled to their burn area; how many miles and for how many hours they'd laboured under the weight of old rubbish saddled to their backs; how slow their progress was to rid themselves of the old.

What a different life. What a strange and foreign land this is. And yet we all have garbage, whether we're from London or Turkey or Iran.

I reboarded the train and took my seat once again. The train attendant hurried to my side as soon as she saw me and smiled at me. She thanked me in her broken English for relinquishing my seat to the man who needed to rest. Her words sounded as tired as she looked, and my heart leaped with compassion for her, travelling this rail line for days, attending to the needs of so many others. *I'd take my job slaving away for the spike-heeled Kimberly any day*, I thought.

As I sat waiting for the other passengers to board and realised we were once again delayed in our departure, I thought about the rubbish-burning men. How light and free they had looked upon ridding themselves of the encumbrances of yesterday's garbage.

The breeze from the open window next to my seat and the memory of the radiant, tired smile of the attendant rested upon me, and I had a momentary spark of inspiration.

If they can burn their trash and leave it behind to be consumed forever by the elements, departing emptied and freed, might I also be able to rid myself of some weight and garbage? And if I did, would I also feel lightened and freed?

I reached into my bag for a pencil. Not finding any blank paper, I settled for a napkin wadded in my pocket. I started a list of names. Each name caused me to recall a grievance I'd suffered from that person, an offense I'd never forgiven, a wrong I had sustained by their hand or deed or word. As if in a trance, without thought for time or day or place, I scribbled and scribbled, filling up one side of the napkin and quickly flipping it over to continue on the other side.

Finishing my list, I set down my pencil. I took a deep breath and went to that quiet place I was still newly discovering, my Hagia Sophia place, and granted forgiveness in my heart to every name on that list.

The train started to move, surprisingly. I had no idea how long I'd been sitting there working on my list. Amazingly, it was long enough that the layover was finished and we were on our way again. As the train picked up speed, I ripped the napkin into bits and shreds and tossed it out the window just as we passed the still-smoking fire pit the men had left. I hoped my list would find the flames, or at least be scorched into nothing by the fiery flames of the sun. I left that list behind me and felt an undeniable sense of liberation. The weight of holding hostage in my heart all those who had wronged me over the years was no longer tying me down. In its place was a cavernous opening of hope and fluttering of delight at how good it felt to have pardoned so many that day for their past crimes against me.

Is it possible to be reborn again and again? If I felt reborn in the Hagia Sophia, I feel even more enlivened now.

I could not believe how heavy I must have been, carrying so much weight in my heart. By forgiving, I had lightened my load. I rested quietly in the new-found peace that came with it, vowing to never again collect the weight of unforgiveness and unrequited penance from those who wronged me.

A strange thing happened then. Somewhere along the border of Turkey and Iran, I realised my seat mates were no longer the older couple who had snored and knitted throughout the first day of our journey. In their place sat a woman with an open seat beside her. She stuck out to me because of her attire. The serviceable, sturdy shoes of peasants, farmers, and nomads from this area were becoming commonplace to me. It was the bright yellow scarf adorning the woman's neck and the bright blue of her fashionable, western-style leather boots that struck me as out of place. It was an odd observation to make, thinking her attire out of the ordinary, since she was dressed precisely the way women at home would dress. I realised how out of place and utterly welcome a sight she was.

The woman glanced over her magazine at me when she sensed my gaze. I smiled apologetically, lifting my hand in a congenial way to indicate I meant no disrespect by staring at her. She smiled in return.

We sat in the companionable silence of two people who don't know each other from Adam but who are saving their acquaintance for a later time, as is prudent for two strangers who will be side by side for two days on a train. We had plenty of time to talk, and so we waited for a later time to do it.

Several hours later, the attendant came by to offer refreshment. I was completely taken aback by the British accent I heard from the woman in the yellow scarf. "Tea, if you have it, please," she requested.

"I will have the same, thank you," I chimed in.

Imagine the unlikely occurrence of two Brits on a train through Iran, sitting side by side to share tea. I still can't believe the coincidence. And I still can't believe I believed in coincidences back then, since this was surely no coincidence. Coincidences rarely are coincidences at all.

Nadine was her name. We talked politely about the weather and our homes and what brought us to this train, like the polite Brits we both were. We didn't pry; we didn't overstep the boundaries of appropriate social etiquette. We spoke in hushed and quiet tones and shared observations from our travels and our hopes for a speedy and comfortable journey to our destinations.

It wasn't until hours later, when we'd exhausted the routine list of topics that are suitable to discuss with a stranger on a train, that we crossed over into deeper conversation. And that was when it happened.

I noticed her hands and how they were clutching a photo of two small children in front of a lopsided birthday cake.

"Are those your children?" I asked my question with a significant tone of respect, since I certainly didn't want her to get the wrong idea about the motivation behind my asking. I wasn't trying to pry, but I felt compelled to hear more about her, her life, her world.

Her gaze dropped to her hands, which were lying clasped in her lap, tangled up with the photo, and I couldn't help but notice her fingers begin to clinch, ever so slightly.

"Yes, they are mine," she said softly, not looking up. "Well, ours, actually. I am married, but I'm not now … oh! It's really a complicated story and not entirely a happy one to share."

Instinctively, I reached to touch her arm in a gesture meant to encourage her to forgive the question and forget it. My fingertips grazed the sleeve of her shirt, and as she continued talking, I was overtaken with the heady realisation that I was hearing her. Not "hearing her" as in the words spoken by her mouth; no, I was "hearing" all the things she wasn't saying. It was as if I were listening to her with a set of ears I'd never used before. She would say one thing, a sort of skimming-the-surface statement about her life, and I would hear the back story simultaneously.

The tale she told was heart-wrenchingly painful to hear, both with the ears on my head and the ears in my heart. She had been forced into hiding in a country like Iran, which so many seek shelter from and not shelter in, by an abusive husband who would search the ends of the earth to locate her and her wealth again. She had been forced to leave her children with him because of issues with obtaining travel visas. This was what I heard when she said the simple words, "I am travelling to Iran for a time, hoping to reconcile my marriage from a safe distance."

The most amazing thing about the two days I spent on the train with Nadine was not the discovery that listening with my heart was a special capability I seemed to have had latent within me. It was that by listening to her, I didn't just have to commiserate and sympathize and then go back to my own life when we parted. Rather, as I listened, I was searching for the words that would help her, the guidance I had within me to share, and the way in which our "coincidental" interaction could be useful for the greater good.

As she finished speaking, I touched her arm again. This time, it was she who was doing the listening as I shared a very short story about some men burning rubbish and the strength and power I'd only recently found through forgiving those who seemed the most undeserving of forgiveness.

The light in Nadine's eyes flickered softly as I spoke, and I knew then that all of our experiences are meant to be shared, not hoarded as we might a secret treasure. It was the most memorable two days I've ever spent – on a train travelling through a war-torn country with a complete stranger as my only companion. In fact, in truth, they were two of the most memorable days of my life, period.

The hug of friendship as we parted and the bounce in her step that I saw as Nadine walked away from me at the train station in Tehran were gifts more precious to me than any I'd ever received. I won't ever forget Nadine.

Six

At World's End

He who lives in harmony with himself,
lives in harmony with the Universe.

—Marcus Aurelius

Matteo

I set up my easels in a square next to the bus station, eagerly waiting for the school across the street to let out for the day. That was when the kids came. Many of them knew me from previous days when I painted with them in the same location. Some would be new faces. Either way, I looked forward to their arrival, along with their scepticism and initial mistrust, which melted away as soon as I put brushes in their hands.

Looking across the street, I watched the doors of the school, anticipating the bell that would soon ring and the opening of those doors. Instead, I saw a woman. She was staring at me. I smiled to her, and to my surprise, she crossed the street and walked towards me.

I hadn't had a date in years, and was thinking I didn't even know how to talk to a woman. I found myself nervous at her approach. *What does she want?*

She laid a hand on an easel, remarking how low to the ground it was. "It's for children," I offered by way of explanation. And then she looked up at me, really looked at me.

Professional clothes, tall-heeled boots, mid-length brown hair, and sparkling blue eyes met my gaze. I knew who she was immediately, before I even picked up on her London accent. *Just like her mother. She's a younger version of her mother.*

We spoke for a while about art and children and my painting and her job. Then she asked if she could stay and meet the children.

As the bell rang and the children flocked to me, my heart became full of hope. I was grateful for one simple fact: coincidences aren't coincidences at all.

Matthew

In the years after, I've often looked back at my journey and marvelled at the way it unfolded. I have to conclude that travel and world exploration are pastimes which every person must adopt, either for leisure or for opportunity to learn from the human condition. No way exists to open our minds and hearts more completely than the inherent chasm of understanding which is created through stepping outside our comfort zone and being present in the reality of another person. I can't think of a better example of this realisation than that which I experienced in the days following my train ride from Istanbul to Tehran.

I said goodbye to Nadine at the train station. As our farewell hug parted and we walked in opposite directions, I was overcome with loneliness. It had been just over one week since I left the sanctuary of my life in London, just over a week since I'd been close to loved ones, my wife and daughter, and I was going to miss the friendship Nadine had brought to my journey.

I was in a low spot, probably feeling sorry for myself and homesick more than anything. In Tehran, a city I'd only seen on the news and in the newspapers, I was an outlander, an absolute stranger to everyone I met, and completely out of my element. Istanbul had definitely felt foreign; Tehran felt even more so. The pulse of Tehran wasn't the old-world charm of Istanbul and the relaxed sense of stability that comes with a country that changes slowly over centuries. No, Tehran vibrated with an edgy and defensive pulse that was evident wherever I looked – in the quickly darting, suspicious eyes of the passers-by, in the piles of rubble that adorned every street, and in the angry slashes of graffiti covering concrete walls and buildings. I could feel the angst in this place.

And who could blame the people of Tehran for exhibiting angst? Theirs was a country constantly torn by war and rumours of war. Theirs was no oasis in the desert. Theirs was a tumultuous hotspot of clashing ideals and bloodshed in the name of conflicting religious ideologies. One only needed to read the news reports coming out of Tehran to know this was the truth.

Before coming to Tehran, I considered myself well travelled. I had interned in Brisbane for a year; I had taken opportunities to holiday in coastal towns all over Europe; I had even visited the USA and Canada. My wife and I had honeymooned in the Caribbean. Still, in hindsight, my travels hadn't been true travels. Instead, they had been a temporary relocation of my same mindset and habits to an environment that was, yes, new to me, but was also where I'd spent more time seeking out the comforts of home (you can find a sturdy cup of English tea wherever you go, if you just look hard enough) than embracing the comforts of a new culture and land. My travels had been limited, in other words, by my own unwillingness to be inconvenienced from my needs long enough to see a new place for what it was.

Tehran yanked me headlong out of that stupor with her raw vibe of chaotic beauty and intensely disparate feel. Tehran was an in-my-face, blatant challenge to everything I thought I knew about travel.

In hindsight, I am grateful for Tehran. This conflicted city showed me that beauty did not exist only in obvious places. Beauty was wherever we chose to look for it. I don't think another city could have taught me this lesson nearly as well. As it ended up, I had many hours in which to walk the streets of the Grand Bazaar, a historic marketplace which dated back to 4000 BCE. I entered the narrow corridors of the bazaar with my set of preconceived expectations based on news coverage I'd seen of this area. I expected a grim, grey, destitute place with even more grim, grey, and destitute people. Nothing could have been further from the truth.

Despite the obvious hardships of the land, politics, and socioeconomic constraints of Iran, I stumbled into a veritable garden of hope. In the bazaar, I was surrounded by ordinary people living ordinary and beautiful lives amid extraordinary circumstances. Similar to a hibiscus I saw blooming next to the train tracks that seemed to flourish and thrive amidst soot, ash, rocks, rubbish, and smog, the Grand Bazaar was a hothouse of exotic desert flowers blooming amid the dearth of their surroundings. My heart was happy to see it. I felt encouraged to be among the proof that my own preconceptions of a war-torn country were blessedly wrong.

As I walked along the bazaar's many corridors and past brick-lined storefronts, the air was infused with spices. I was delighted by scents of cardamom and cinnamon. I bought a cup of tea from a hawker carrying an oversized kettle, and marvelled that this thin-framed man with hollow cheeks was able to manage the weight of it without spilling a drop, all the while navigating the crowds with a smile on his face. As I sipped my tea and smiled appreciatively at the man, he began to talk to me in short spurts of rudimentary English. I learned he made about 20,000 tomans each day ($15) by selling tea in the morning and lemon sorbet in the afternoon. I asked him if this salary was enough to survive on, and he replied that it was a difficult living. Then he smiled with his eyes in a universally recognized gesture stemming from a father's love and added that it didn't matter how hard he had to work; he was saving for the dowry of his daughter and hoping it would be enough to see her married well. I bought another cup of tea and paid the man double for it, explaining that I too had a daughter and understood how motivating it could be to slave the day away in order to prepare for her future. I don't think he understood my words, but bowed humbly in gratitude for the money I had given him.

There were many things I saw in Tehran that soothed me, comforted me, made me feel like a part of humanity bigger than my own immediate family and friends. I left the bazaar with a deep sense of belonging to something that pulsed and vibrated with love, human virtue, and peace. The commonality of being part of the human race was beautiful, and strangely visible in even the most dour of places.

On my way to the airport, I considered how misleading the evening news could be. I felt sad inside that the only reflection the reports shared were those of an ugly, angry Tehran, not the beautiful one I had encountered that day.

I arrived at the airport in plenty of time for the flight to Ulaanbaatar, Mongolia. As I had come to expect, I hit another travel snag. Prepared for a reservation to be in place, I was told my reservation was non-existent, and air travel out of Iran was limited due to recent political unrest.

I didn't complain, I didn't balk, and I didn't dig my heels in.

The road to Hong Kong was one I knew by now wouldn't be paved smoothly. And honestly, I would have been surprised if my further travel had gone down without a hiccup. It wasn't the way this journey was unfolding. I was resigned to it now.

Instead of asking exasperated questions of "Why?" and "When?" and "How?" of the staff at the airport, I simply sighed and asked for information on my options. I did not resist; I went with the flow. It was a new concept for me, but one I felt increasingly capable of embracing.

And that was how I ended up on a boat. I was resigned to my fate of travelling to Hong Kong via the longest route possible.

My stomach was in knots from the day I had spent walking the streets of Tehran, both in the bazaar and in the residential areas surrounding it. Challenging myself to be absorbed by Tehran's people and way of life, instead of being only a picture-taking tourist, I'd eaten street food. *Doogh* – a dried mint and sheep's-milk yogurt beverage – flatbread wrapping a skewer of grilled meat, and a savoury rice and meat dish I was told contained cow's stomach, rested heavily in my belly as I lay on the bed in the sleeping compartment of the boat. The fragrances of the streets were unforgettable though, and I had no regrets about the potpourri of foods I'd tasted amid the carts and shops spilling their fragrances of simmering stews and quince preserves into the sultry heat. It had been a sensory day to remember, and I was glad to have two weeks on a boat to spend digesting all I'd enjoyed.

As I lay in bed, considering my time in Tehran and listening to the upset of my stomach, I casually laid my hand on my belly. My hand was drawn there by some invisible cord I could not have named if I tried and could not have denied if I'd wanted to. I was comforted by the warmth coming from my hand and let it linger there. I closed my eyes and visualized the warmth sinking deep into the tissues of my stomach, appeasing its discord.

In my mind's eye, I visualized a world map, noting that Tehran was due west from my final destination, Hong Kong. Since travelling the way the crow flies had failed me yet again, I was on a boat en route to Myanmar, which used to be known as Burma. The only problem with the boat journey was that there was a land mass in the way, preventing the journey from being a straight route east. That land mass was India.

I opened the orientation pamphlet in my cabin and traced my finger along the boat route we were embarking on, noting that I'd be sailing the Indian Ocean for the first time from the mid-range accommodations of an ocean liner. The thought was thrilling and exotic and adventurous and exhilarating all at the same time.

The days and nights passed quickly. In between dressing for meals and walking the decks when the weather was nice, I had a lot of time on my hands. I read and wrote letters back home which I knew wouldn't post for a long time to come. In fact, I'd probably be home again long before the letters arrived from what felt like an outpost at the world's end. I met some of the other passengers, but most were travelling for leisure and we simply didn't seem to have much of a connection. I didn't want to trouble them with my sad story of seeking a way to help my daughter while they were jubilantly enjoying their holiday. So I kept to myself mostly.

Though my accommodations were comfortable, I was cold and achy all over from nights of sleeping in a bed that rocked with the sea. The sea breeze was deceptive – while my shut-in cabin craved a fresh breeze from opening my windows, the air was cool, and I awoke with neck cramps and joints which weren't used to the chill and the jostling of the boat.

I couldn't recall a time I'd had so much free time on my hands. It was strange and alien to me. I found myself slowing down to nearly a complete stop. Before, I would never have been comfortable sitting in the same spot for hours, staring at the distant waves, but this quickly became my favourite pastime. With my eyes fixed on a distant spot, my mind's eye wandered, turning images over and over and examining memories and conversations from days, weeks, months, and years in the past. I continued my practice of jotting down names daily and shredding them into the ocean after forgiving the owners of those names in my heart.

Sitting, thinking quietly, and forgiving became a daily routine and one I looked forward to. With it, I noticed a heightened awareness come upon me. There on a boat, at what felt like the world's end, I became aware not only of my body and its positioning, stresses, and strengths; I also became aware of ways to effect change in myself.

I became fascinated by the heat I felt coming from my hand. Sometimes I would sense a simmering under the skin that tingled. Sometimes it was just steady heat I could feel only when I placed my hand next to a cooler area of my body. When I placed my hands with palms facing one another and only inches apart, I was amazed at the sense of pull between them, as if there were strands of energy bouncing between my palms. As I pulsed my hands back and forth in a yo-yo motion, it felt as if I were playing with that energy and stretching, pulling, retracting it by the movement of my hands.

I must have looked silly to the other passengers. My hair had grown quite shaggy and looked unkempt most days. My travel wardrobe was woefully devoid of clean clothes. I didn't remember the last time I had shaved. To passengers walking by, I must've looked positively mad. But I was drawn so inwardly by then with my daily quiet times and practice of forgiving and mulling through the contents of my brain, I simply didn't care what I looked like. I was in the throes of self-discovery in an all-encompassing way, in a way which ensnared me in a world of my own making.

If someone had walked up to me and snapped their fingers next to my ear, I doubt I would've heard them walking close or snapping at all, so engulfed I was in an inner dialogue of discovery.

By far the most fascinating thing I discovered on my boat ride around the southern tip of India was the heat and energy emanating from my hands. By trial and error I experimented with hovering them over spots on my body which I sensed to be weaker or aching or otherwise unwell. Closing my eyes and concentrating only on the heat I was directing from my hands, I found I was able to appease my achy joints, settle my stomach after a bout of seasickness, and unravel the tension in my head and neck from a night spent sleeping on the rocking sea. It was an amazing discovery. The more I experimented, the more fascinated I was by what seemed to be an ability to heal myself using only my hands and my mental concentration.

One day, after a morning spent in quiet contemplation and hovering my hands over my torso and limbs for at least an hour, I realised how lonely I was. I was entering an area of my existence I'd never experienced before. I wanted desperately to share my new-found healing abilities with someone who cared about me. I was excited and a bit stunned too, and wished I had a friend to share it all with.

I thought of my wife then, how she had desperately clung to every traditional healing method she could find to help our daughter. I wondered how she'd feel about letting me try to lay my hands on our daughter instead. Surely she would laugh. But we were both so desperate for our daughter to heal that perhaps she would be open to my trying it. I wished I could know what her reaction would be.

I thought of trying to make a friend on the boat. I considered introducing myself to another tourist, someone who might be accepting of a frumpy traveller like me with a strange new experience to share. But alas, I feared the rejection and laughter I knew would ensue.

As I sat on a deck in the sun one afternoon, puzzling over my need for friendship and wondering where to find it, I recalled an image as clear as day. It was the image of a dapper man leaning over a beautiful woman, gifting her with a watch. Could it have been a scant two weeks prior when I had seen that ad in a magazine on my flight from London to Istanbul? Time was moving so slowly, and so much was happening to me with each passing day that the memory of the advertisement seemed something from a prior lifetime. But yes, it had been only two weeks ago.

I remembered then how I had gotten what I wished for when I verbalized my desire for a train. I wondered if it would work again now if I verbalized my desire for a friend. I closed my eyes and pictured Nadine, recalling the fondness I had for her and the companionship we'd shared over the course of two days on a train. I felt gratitude for her friendship welling up in my heart. Silently, I mouthed the words, "I desire friendship on my travels, someone I can share my experiences with for their greater good and mine."

Feeling as though I'd done all I could, wondering if a friend would materialize out of nowhere or days later or at all, I spent the rest of the afternoon enjoying the rocking of the boat, contemplating the rise and fall of each wave I spotted, and anticipating my arrival in Myanmar.

Seven

On the Brink

Compassion is beyond all description.

—Guru Nanak Dev Ji

Elle

I sat in a coffee shop, at a table with a waterfront view, and sipped slowly from a steaming ceramic mug. Though coffee was my usual choice of beverage on a chilly day, I had ordered herbal tea instead and gratefully inhaled the aroma of chamomile and peppermint. I needed to relax. I needed to calm down. I needed to think.

The day had started out well, as they all had since moving to Stockholm, but had ended in such sudden turmoil that I was left reeling with emotion. My heart felt wrung out and my legs still failed to steady me, hours after the event that had changed the course of my day. *Changed the course of my life?*

My superior was a seasoned attorney with a focus on family law. That's really all I knew about him. He was old school, from a time when employees were on a need-to-know basis and superiors didn't dally in water-cooler talk with subordinates about weekend plans, family life, or their interests and hobbies. I hadn't thought this strange since, like most attorneys I'd come to know, my boss, Jon, worked constantly. I simply assumed he didn't have time for a non-work life.

I'd been made to sign a confidentiality agreement as my work began in support of Jon and his latest trial case. I'd busied myself researching precedent cases and gathering documentation and copying and typing and generally making myself supportive of my boss in all ways.

On the day of the trial, I discovered Jon had left behind on his desk the case file we'd tirelessly worked to compile (at the expense of weekends, sleep, and opportunities to do my laundry and go to the market, I might add).

I hailed a cab and offered double the fare if the driver would speed through traffic lights and get me to the courthouse in record time, which he did. As I climbed the steps, I saw my boss standing for an interview with a group of excited reporters jamming microphones in his face. I hung back and watched.

"Will there be justice for Mr Ferar today?" The voice of one reporter shouted above the rest, and she directed her question at my boss.

"Indeed, there will. My client is innocent of the charges against him, and soon the court will reach the same conclusion. Good day." Jon caught my eye as he turned to retreat from the crowd of reporters. He signalled for me to advance. I handed him the folder, which he thanked me for, and watched as he rushed inside.

I stood perfectly still then, watching Jon retreat into the courthouse.

I went down to the employee lounge and grabbed the day's newspaper and saw the face of Aarone Ferrar on the front page with a knee-weakening caption underneath it.

Mega star pleads not guilty to charges of brutal child abuse leading to death of infant daughter.

I took the paper back to my desk and read the article. A harrowing realisation sunk in. I began to weep silently. I don't know how long I sat there, but it must have been several hours. The sunken feeling in my stomach wouldn't let me rise from my chair, especially not with the realisation of what I had done.

Hours later, a phone call came. I answered it and heard Jon's voice over the din of many loud voices in the background.

"Elle! You did great getting me that file! And all the months of work you've put into this case! It all paid off! We won, Elle! We won!"

Superstar Aarone Ferar had been cleared of child abuse charges and his remaining children had been returned to him. The only problem was, the man was as guilty as could be, but a savvy legal loophole had freed him from retribution. And I had been there the whole time to assist in making it all happen.

Sitting in the coffee shop, I reviewed the day's events and sank deeper into my chair. I thought I'd been helpful, I had applauded myself for the professionalism and efficiency with which I'd assisted Jon. And now, three tiny children were returning home to an abusive father, maybe even this very minute.

A quiet male voice at my shoulder returned me from the sea of regret I'd been drowning in, and I realised the kind waiter was asking if I needed more tea. He was a different waiter than the one who originally had taken my order, and I recognized his voice immediately: the man from the school, with all the easels.

I nodded gravely at his repeated question of whether I wanted more tea, and smiled weakly at him as I returned to my waterfront view. The compassion I felt for the three children I'd never meet and the regret that welled up in me at the inability to change my involvement in their fate was crippling. Soon, I would have to make a decision. I sat quietly and sipped, weighing my options.

Matthew

In the morning, we docked in Puri, a coastal town in India. I listened with interest as the boat's tourism manager described the Hindu traditions surrounding this ancient seaport. She was a short, bland-looking woman who weebled and wobbled from foot to foot as she spoke, reminding me of an egg balanced precariously on its head.

"We will not be stopping here for long, just enough time to stretch your legs on the white sand beach and take in the sights of the fishermen and shops. This is a special place,

Puri. Not only is it one of the oldest cities in eastern India, it is one of the four holiest points of pilgrimage for Hindus. Traditionally, Puri was seen as a holy place to die, though I hope none of you will try it out." She laughed nervously and the crowd chuckled.

"We will take on new passengers here. I regret to inform you we will not be here long enough for you to visit any of the temples or shrines, though there are some old and lovely ones to be seen. I hope you will enjoy your short stay in Puri. We take to the water again in the mid-afternoon."

Despite the obvious disappointment that there seemed to be much to see in Puri I wouldn't have time for, I was simply relieved to be off the boat and standing on solid ground for the first time in days. I thought I might shop a bit and perhaps pick up scarves or incense for my wife. Pocketing some cash and stowing the rest of my funds, passport, and travel documents in the safe, I joined the throngs of my boat mates and moved slowly down the stairs of the ship's hold to the exit.

The beaches of Puri were certainly lovely, as the travel manager had suggested. The sparkling white sand looked almost like fresh-fallen snow in the morning light and I paused to admire it, letting the other anxious tourists pass me by. I sat on a driftwood log and soaked in the rays of sunlight and gazed with interest at the fishing boats hauling in their morning catch.

I marvelled at the simple work of fishing to support an existence. The men I saw, their skin weathered from sun and their hands calloused from working the nets and rods and ropes of their trade, seemed so peaceful, so serene. It was an interesting dichotomy to view their occupation in comparison to my own, which, as I reminded myself, I would soon have to return to. The demanding Kimberly would likely have filled and overfilled my inbox by now, and the laborious toils of my career waited.

More than just the difference in how these men looked while they worked, I couldn't help but notice how different our goals were in our work. For me, if I worked hard and didn't get myself fired, I could expect a pay cheque at the end of every week. If I repeated this for years and years, I might get a raise or a promotion, which might lead to stock options or additional vacation time. For these men, the outcome of their labours was nothing they could anticipate. They simply presented themselves to the sea every day and hoped their daily catch would be enough to sell in the market for a wage they could exchange for food for their family. If their catch was small, they might be forced to bring home only a few fishes, instead of being able to buy vegetables or fruits or other staples.

They go to the sea, they don't know what they'll find, and they somehow trust that their efforts will be enough to feed their family for that day.

I stood to walk away from the tide and follow my fellow ship guests to the village. Shaking my head, I realised how difficult it must be to exist and simply trust that your needs and your family's needs would be provided for. I thought of the turmoil of jockeying for career advancement and opportunities to outshine my peers in boardroom brawls. I thought of the ever-present, underlying fire in my belly, prompting me to work more, work harder, work later, work earlier, and make more money so that I could give my family … more.

But how much is enough and where does it end?

I pictured myself as a fisherman then. I laughed to myself. *If I were a fisherman, I'd be the kind who rowed his boat out to the ocean and demanded the largest fish present themselves and jump into the boat. I might also pick a fight with the other fishermen and try to muscle them out of the best fishing spots.*

All I could conclude then was that fishing was either not what I was cut out for, or that somehow I needed to think more on this concept of bringing a fisherman's mentality into my career life.

In the village, shops were opening for the day; shopkeepers were pulling down the barricades that had shielded their goods from the ocean mist, humidity, and salt of the night. Vendors of scarves and bags, incense, candles, and postcards all vied to be the store of choice for the throngs of tourists our boat had brought to shore. I stood back, watching the activities and observing money being exchanged for trinkets and trifles. I wanted to shop for my wife, but I was not in any hurry to join the masses of grabbing, jostling tourists.

As I walked through the narrow streets, a boy caught my eye. He was without a shirt, and his mop of scruffy brown hair looked unwashed and matted. The sun gleamed on the dark tan of his skin, and I looked down to the bottom of his ripped, dingy trousers to notice he was barefoot.

He was calling out something to the passers-by, something in a language I didn't understand, and motioning to the tin can he held in his hand.

A beggar, I thought. *No matter where you go, someone's always begging.*

I placed my hand in my pocket as I passed, intending to select a small bill to give to the boy from the fold of money I'd stowed there. As I pulled my hand out of my pocket and looked down to begin sorting through my bills, the beggar raced towards me. Bumping into my side, he had come at me with such speed that I almost didn't know what hit me. I saw him racing down the adjacent alleyway and noticed with dismay that my entire fold of bills was gone from my hand.

That little beggar took all my money!

I gave chase down the same alley, my legs enjoying the stretching motion I'd denied them for these last weeks of being cooped up in various modes of transportation. They felt rested and strong, and despite the fact that I hoped they would take me right to the boy who'd robbed me, I felt appreciative of the exercise whether it helped me get my money back or not.

Through winding alleys and over obstacles of rubbish bins, avoiding pitfalls of slippery cabbage leaves and animal waste, I chased the boy. I kept close behind him, watching with a primitive awareness to know which turns he took. And then I lost him.

I turned right; he wasn't anywhere to be seen. I turned left; there was no sign of him.

I was in an open courtyard, a residential area that showed a line of tightly packed, neatly kept hovels dug from the rocks. Bright curtains covered the doorways and windows hewn from sandstone, and a simple fountain gurgled in the middle of the court amid well-tended beds of flowers. I smelled incense seeping from the residences. I knelt down by the fountain and splashed water from the spirited trickle onto my face, appreciating the gentle sound of water springing from the earth and falling back down.

A hand rested on my shoulder. I turned to see a man in business attire and shined shoes looking down on me. He had a navy-blue turban on his head, and the colour accentuated his eyes and the dark skin of his face.

"Sir, please, come with me." The man's voice was articulate and inviting.

"What? Who are you? What is it you want?" I was tired from my exertion and in no mood to be distracted from the frustrated feeling welling up inside me that reminded me I'd just been robbed.

"I have the criminal, the perpetrator of the crime against you. I know where he went."

"Oh, I see! Well, yes, okay. Let's go to him!" I replied.

The man turned his back on me and walked a few paces to one of the hovels in the courtyard, sweeping through the scarlet curtain covering the door and returning a brief moment later with the shirtless boy from the market, held immobilized by the man's hand gripping his ear.

"Is this he? Is this the dishonourable boy who has thieved you?"

I walked closer, though I knew already this was the same boy. I looked into the boy's eyes. Their chocolate brown melted under my gaze. I realised then that this boy could be no more than 5 or 6 years old. I laid my hand on his shoulder and deepened my gaze. The compassion I felt for him was arresting, and my heart heard what his words had not spoken.

To be sure I heard correctly, I stepped behind him and peered through the window of the hovel the boy had stepped from seconds ago. There, as I suspected, lay a greyish man sleeping under a tattered blanket, breathing laboriously.

"Well? Is it him?" The businessman's voice was demanding and I turned to address him.

"How did you find him? I chased him for so long and couldn't keep up," I answered.

"I saw the boy steal from you and I know his family. I came to his home to wait and, as I expected, he showed up a moment later. What shall we do with him? The town's elders will surely want to punish him."

At the sound of the word *punish*, the boy began to squirm, anxious to get away. The businessman only refortified his grip on the boy's ear.

"Let him go," I said calmly.

"What? Let him go? But sir, this boy has deeply wronged you and he must be punished!" The protest of the businessman was authoritative and commanding.

"I said, let him go."

"And your money? Here." He reached out the wad of mixed currency notes and I took it. "At least you can have your money back. I will speak with the boy's father. The boy will be punished."

The businessman turned on his heel, releasing the boy into the grip of my hand on his arm, and moved as if to re-enter the hovel.

"No, no, please. There is no need," I said quietly.

The boy paused in his struggles and looked up at me. I opened his hand with my own and placed the bills into it.

His gaze met mine and he smiled, releasing a sea of words into the damp morning air which I sensed must be something along the lines of thanks and appreciation.

The boy grabbed my hand and placed several of the bills back into it. He spoke another stream of words and the businessman translated.

"The boy says, 'Many thanks to you, kind man. I am returning to you what is beyond my need for the day. Today I needed food and medicine for my father. Thank you for your provision and your mercy.'"

My heart welled with gratitude for this experience and I was moved to reach again for the boy's hand, returning the crumpled bills to his keeping. "I am happy to give it to you. Thank you for accepting my gift."

I turned to walk away from the boy and the businessman and aimed my steps back towards the ship. As I walked, the businessman caught up with me.

"You are going to the ship, are you not?"

"Yes," I said, "I am ready to move on from this place now."

"I will walk with you. I am a new passenger on the ship and am embarking here to continue with it as it journeys to Myanmar." The man's legs were longer than my own, and I noticed he had to pace himself to keep from walking ahead of me.

We walked together without speaking. Finally, he broke the silence.

"Why did you do it, sir? Why did you leave your money with the boy? It is not acceptable in this culture for stealing to go unpunished, yet you refused to command his punishment. Why?" The pleading in the man's voice was genuine but not judgemental; he seemed curious more than anything.

"Tell me, what is your name and how is it that you know this boy's family?" I asked quietly.

"I am Devinder. I'm a Sikh. I'm a businessman originally from Punjab. I own many companies there, but long ago, I lived here, in Puri. The boy is well known to me; his father is a friend of my family. This is how I know that Hindus look grievingly upon theft. It is not tolerated."

I looked up at him and stopped walking. I wanted to see his eyes as he answered my next question.

"And tell me, Devinder, what is it that ails the boy's father?"

"He was a fisherman. His boat capsized in a storm. He spent days fighting for his life on the open ocean before finally being washed to shore. He can no longer fish for his family. He will die soon, like his wife before him. The boy is his only son."

I closed my eyes, listening to the inner truth I had discovered only this afternoon, revelling in its beauty and breathing deeply as I prepared to share it with this man.

"Devinder ..." I started.

"Please, call me Dev. Everyone does."

I placed my hands on his shoulders and peered into his eyes.

"Dev, sometimes in our life and work, we are the fishermen, working and preparing and slaving to make ends meet for those we care for. But sometimes, we also have to let ourselves be the fish. We have to give whatever we have to meet the immediate needs of those who need it, like the fish who give their lives to sustain and nourish others. I let myself be the fish today, Dev. The fish don't require punishment of the fishermen any more than I required punishment of this boy. Hopefully the fish I gave will help feed this boy and his father for many days to come."

Dev listened. His lips crept into a smile and a light filled his eyes. We started walking again in the direction of the ship. Our steps fell into a comfortable pace, and we soon reached the dock.

"I've told you my name, sir, but I don't think I caught yours." We set foot on the plank, and I turned to look at him as I answered.

"My name is Matthew." I smiled, wondering if by some miracle this was the friend I had attracted to myself. "And where are you going to again, Dev? What is the purpose of your journey?"

He didn't answer right away, as if measuring the silence to see how accepting I would be of the answer that was the truth.

"I am going to Hong Kong, Matthew, by way of Myanmar. There is an answer I seek there, in Lantau." His words were spoken quietly but with a fair amount of hesitation. Surely he suspected I would press for more information, that I would want to know why someone was travelling to Lantau, and that I would have many, many questions about what answers he was seeking.

I simply smiled, though, and continued to board the boat. There was no need to reply right away. We had many more miles to travel together, and we would have many opportunities to talk further about his journey. I glanced back at him and replied, "How wonderful and … how interesting."

As I lay in my cabin that night, I suddenly recalled that the day's turn of events had kept me from purchasing a souvenir for my wife. I knew she would understand. I had an aching then that the healing in my hands was finding difficult to abate. I ached to see my wife, to share with her all of the experiences I'd been having, and to give her encouragement that today, finally, I had learned the value of living as the fishermen do.

Eight

To Hear, to Help, to See

Each of us is interlocked with an undeniable creative energy that constitutes the world around us. You are an irreplaceable part of the whole.

—Mann Matharu

Matthew

The journey onward from Puri was pleasant and unexpected. Though my days were fraught with concern for my daughter, the twinge I had previously felt upon all thoughts of her was different now. Gone was the weighty thud in my heart and the searing pain of guilt I had felt at the thought of being responsible for her accident. Gone too were the unfettered anxiety and palpitations of angst I had felt at the realisation that I had originally hoped to have been to Hong Kong and back again by now. Certainly I was as concerned for her recovery as ever; certainly I was burdened by the direness of her situation; certainly I was longing for news of her condition. But the burden wasn't distracting me to the point of delirium the way it had before. Now, in place of a set of emotions and worry I could not contain, I held the same level of love and concern for my daughter in my heart, but continued my journey with solidarity, steadfastness, and resolve.

Dev proved to be the greatest of distractions. His friendship not only kept me company throughout the remainder of our trip by boat around the coast of India, but also carried me forward in what I was beginning to recognize was a journey into my own depths.

We spent several days sharing meals and taking walks around the boat deck, during which time we spoke amiably about all kinds of topics. I continued to look for an opportunity to ask about the purpose of his travel. The coincidence that we were both travelling to Lantau hadn't escaped me, and I was curious to know more. I considered approaching the topic many times, but something always held me back.

When I was a child growing up in London, I spent an afternoon playing hide-and-seek with my sister. She was several years older than me and didn't usually want to spend any time with me at all. However, on one afternoon, a particularly long rainy spell had kept us both indoors for several days and she, growing quite bored, acquiesced to playing a game with me. As we ran about our flat, taking turns hiding and seeking, I vowed to find the very best hiding place ever, one in which she would never find me. But I ended up doing more finding than hiding, as it turned out.

I scurried into the back of my parents' closet and stood inside my father's boots, my body draped in a long coat, and prepared to wait for what I felt sure would be an extraordinarily long period of time until she found me. There was no way my sister would find me in that spot quickly. As I waited, I felt the walls and floors of the closet with my hands, growing bored with maintaining my hiding. To my complete surprise, I came upon a large box I had never seen before. Opening it, I found brightly wrapped gifts with my and my sister's names on them. I had found our Christmas presents, neatly wrapped and awaiting delivery by "Santa Claus" in a few short weeks.

I burst out of the closet then, completely ruining my hiding place, and proceeded to rip open the packages and reveal the gifts underneath. My sister came to my side and joined in as well. In short order, we sat amid scraps of ripped wrapping paper and our gifts from Santa, just as my father walked into the room.

I will never forget the look on his face. Surprisingly, he wasn't angry with us. He smiled a sort of lopsided grin, as if he completely understood that children cannot resist the urge to seek and find gifts and rip into them with utter abandon when given the chance. He sat us down next to him on the bed and put his arms around us. Then he spoke.

"Children, there are some things in life you can never replace. Now, in this moment, I hope you realize that you can never go back to the beautiful mystery of wondering what your gifts contain. And you can never go back to the innocent time when you thought Santa Claus existed. By your actions, you've led yourself across that bridge and burned it behind you. I hope it was worth it." His eyes were sad then, as if he'd been forced to reveal to us one of the most weighty facts of life and hadn't enjoyed having to be the one to do it.

I felt that way again, just like that small boy, when I spent time with Dev. Some part of me resisted pressing him for more information about the purpose of his travels. It was as if, once I asked the question, I would never be able to go back to not knowing the answer. And somehow I suspected that knowing the answer would take me far away from a simpler, natural, and innocent place.

For days and days, I resisted the urge to ask Dev why he was going to Lantau. I willed myself to be content with simply knowing that he was going there, willed myself to be content with not knowing why. Sometimes the questions are more useful than the answers.

As time passed on our boat, I put away the temptation of asking Dev about his trip by being an active listener. In the same way I had listened to Nadine with my heart on the train from Istanbul to Tehran, I set to the task of listening to Dev. What I found was that this man was an enigma to me on the one hand, and a complete mirror image of myself on the other.

Dev presented himself with flourish every day, adorned with careful and precise clothing, and gave the outer impression of being a successful businessman. What I heard when I listened with my heart was another story.

Dev was successful, to be sure. His net worth far exceeded that of any man or woman I'd ever personally known. He dealt in acquisitions, buying up failing companies in the Middle East and rebuilding them from the inside out into profitable corporations. The empire beneath his feet covered the gamut of industries: he had a hand in everything from textiles to oil to agriculture and tourism. He was proud of what he'd accomplished and built at such a tender age. In his young 28 years, Dev was, in all honesty, as prosperous as I had dreamed of being.

When I looked at Dev, I was stirred with a bit of jealousy. His wealth alone was enviable, but more than that, I envied his drive and energy and youth. He had everything I'd ever wanted to have, everything I'd ever wanted to be able to give to my family. I recognized myself in him. Or at least, in him I recognized the self I wanted to be.

And yet Dev was not all he seemed. At dinner one night, I watched as he held his head in his hands. Thinking he'd perhaps had too much wine, I leaned across the table to lay a hand on his shoulder and inquire whether he needed to retire for the evening to rest. As I brushed his shoulder, I realised the truth about Dev in a flash of insight.

The only son of a sheepherder, Dev had been raised in the dry, dusty hills of India. Despite his eagerness to learn the trade of his father, Dev was a constant disappointment to his parents. He lost sheep, he couldn't keep track of them, and the family's finances were affected by his negligence.

His father was a hard man. Amid a rain of verbal abuse and rants from his father, who cursed and made sure young Dev knew he would never amount to anything, Dev ran away from home at 16. His existence as a man was shaped by his desire to overcome the low expectations of a father who had never showed him love or affection.

Dev needed money and power and prestige. He needed his business empire to be of such great worth and influence that news of it would reach the ends of the earth, including a small shanty in the hills of India where his parents still resided. He needed his father to know that he had defied the curse and made something of himself. Dev would do anything, go to any lengths, to make sure he owned more of the world than any other man.

It consumed him.

I looked at him there across the table and saw him in a new light. Beyond the façade of youth and wealth sat a little boy who had withered and diminished from lack of a father's love. The compassion I felt for him then was exorbitant.

"Dev, your head is bothering you, is it?" I asked casually, not wanting to let on all that I had seen and heard of his sad tale as I'd sat there listening to him with my heart.

"Oh, yes, I suppose it is. I have a steady pounding in my head all the time, truth be told. Being on this boat is particularly hard, and I've been hurting more than usual." His voice sounded tired and so very weary.

"What is it about the boat that bothers you?" I ventured my question cautiously, but with a tone of concern.

"I'm just so far away from everything here. I need to be able to watch my stock prices and get the financial forecasts. My empire could be crumbling around me and I wouldn't even know it!" Dev spoke the last sentence loudly and stood up suddenly, pushing his chair back. "I think I'll go lie down."

"Wait, Dev. I think I can help. Please, will you sit back down and let me try?" I stood and motioned with my hands to his chair.

He sat once again. I stood behind him, letting my hands rest on either side of his head, at his temples.

In my heart, I pictured a boyish version of Dev. I considered his past and the failings of his father; I imagined the everyday chaos of a man who owned much of the Middle East and presided over a financial empire rivalling that of a king. I willed my hands to dispense comfort and healing, to carry my heartfelt desire that Dev live a long, full, happy life, devoid of the baggage his father had left him with. I came into my Hagia Sophia quiet place and pictured Dev walking through a serene field of green grass and fragrant flowers, adorned in simple clothing, without the shimmer and sparkle of his cufflinks and expensive watch. Instead, in my mind's eye, Dev was smiling and happy and free, chasing children while grasping the hand of a woman who loved him with all her heart.

In all honesty, I didn't know what I was doing. I simply was imagining an alternate future for Dev, one that would give the man some peace from his aching head and the weight of an empire on his shoulders. It wasn't that I necessarily thought he should have a doting wife and kids – God knew that brought a set of headaches all its own. I only felt compassion for the man whose wealth and career were quite obviously driving him to an early grave.

"Mmmmmm, wow …" Dev's voice returned me from my quiet place to the hustle and bustle of the dining room. "My headache is gone!"

"So glad to hear it!" I replied.

"No, you don't understand. I've had that headache literally for years. How did you make it go away so quickly?" The tone of Dev's voice was one of a man who was supremely confused by what he'd just witnessed.

"I … well, I'm not sure, really. I was just trusting my instinct, I guess." I had surprised myself too.

The next day, we finally disembarked at Myanmar. As I left the boat for the last time, I found myself puzzling over the changes Dev had brought to my perspective. Instead of thinking of Dev as a younger version of myself, career-minded and bent on financial gain, I looked at him now as I imagine others must've looked at me several short weeks ago. I felt sorry for Dev, for the prison his career goals had put him in. I left our boat wishing with all my heart that he, like I seemed to have been able to do in such a short time, could overcome the limiting thought that wealth was the source of all happiness.

I waited at the dock for the bus that would transport the passengers to the travel station, where the hordes of people I'd shared space with the last couple of weeks would disperse and go in a myriad of different ways. My sparse luggage was gathered around me and I craned my neck, looking this way and that for signs of Dev. I hadn't seen him since dining with him the evening before, and I wondered how his head was feeling today. Not seeing him, I roosted on my suitcase, taking the opportunity to sit down and rest while I waited for the bus.

I glanced down at the dock. The piers supporting it were covered with green sea growth and barnacles. I noticed a smallish spot on the dock. Standing and walking towards it, I stooped down for a closer look. The spot was an insect, a tiny bumblebee lying on her side. Thinking she must be dead, I stood to return to my luggage but was stopped by the very slightest perception that the bee was twitching her wing. I stooped down again and scooped the bee into my palm, raising it to eye level.

I looked at the bee and saw her wings slightly twitch. I set my finger down beside her. She crawled onto it ever so slowly. I realised in that moment that she wasn't injured; she was simply tired. Her arduous journey was far and she was too exhausted to finish it.

I walked over to a planter of flowers and attempted to let her climb onto one, but she stubbornly refused to leave my finger. Fishing in my pocket, I withdrew a packet of honey that I had taken from the dining room, thinking I'd use it to make a cup of tea in my room the night before. I squeezed a drop of honey into my palm and scooted the bee down my finger towards it. The bee's two black antennae began to twitch, and her small, pinkish tongue made contact with the drop. I waited patiently while she ate from my hand.

A crowd gathered around me, watching with curiosity at my strange actions. I don't think anyone had ever seen a frumpy, weary traveller feed a bee from his hand. Dev was at the front of the crowd, arms crossed.

Amid the chaos of the boat dock, the sounds of bells and whistles and shouts from dock workers, the crowd around me was quiet as could be. I looked up at the faces staring at me and noted the genuine interest in the eyes of the onlookers. I smiled and held up my hand, to help even those in the back see the tiny body on my palm.

"She was too weary to finish her journey. A little sustenance should give her a lift!"

The crowd smiled and nodded, watching and waiting.

After about twenty minutes, without any warning, the bee suddenly took flight, her wings beating frantically and lifting her into the sky. She flew away in the blink of an eye.

The crowd cheered and applauded. Never in my life did I think I'd be standing on the dock of a foreign land, among a throng of strangers smiling ear to ear at having revived a bumblebee. The joy I felt in that moment was worth more than all the gold in Dev's empire to me. Gone was my jealousy of his wealth and any wish to work as long and hard as he had to prove myself to anyone. Instead, being here and being part of the journey of a tiny member of our big world felt more right than anything I'd done in a long time. And I didn't think it at all prideful or arrogant to recognize that without me, the little bee would surely have perished.

Nine

Every Human, Beast, and Bug

It is only with the heart that one can see rightly;
what is essential is invisible to the eye.

—Antoine de Saint-Exupery

Matthew

"Matthew! Matthew, over here!" Dev's voice was barely audible above the noise of the crowd on the dock. I glanced up, thinking I'd heard my name.

"Dev? Ah, there you are! I was wondering if I would see you here this morning." I shook hands warmly with my friend and then reached down to grab my baggage. "How is your head? How are you feeling?" We started moving in the direction of the buses.

Dev smiled. "Just fine! Great! I feel amazing today!"

"I'm glad to hear it," I said. "So, since it sounds like we're aimed in the same direction, towards Hong Kong, will you be on the bus with me, the one leaving at five tonight?"

"No, no, no, my friend. I won't be taking a bus to Hong Kong." Dev paused and let his words drift into the morning breeze.

I was disappointed to hear we wouldn't be travelling together. I had enjoyed having a friend to travel with.

"I see. Well, I guess this is farewell, then?" I asked.

Instead of replying, Dev changed the subject. "I was thinking I might squeeze in a quick trip over to the Shwedagon Paya this morning. You know, the Buddhist temple. Want to come along?"

"I can't imagine being in Myanmar without seeing it. Yes! Yes, I'd love to go!" I had read about the Shwedagon Paya in a travel book. It was one of Buddhism's most sacred sites. Eight hairs from the Buddha were thought to be enshrined there in a temple of gold.

Dev and I took a taxi to the towering temple that was a prominent presence in the city of Yangon. We spent the morning walking the terraces and grounds of the beautiful Buddhist temple, marvelling at the way it had sustained centuries of political and religious upheaval, earthquakes, and the passage of time. The contemplative silence of the devout, gathered to meditate at the feet of the glorious bronze Buddha statues, was lulling, and our conversation lapsed in response.

Dev was muted in a way I hadn't seen before. His usual energy and exuberance were lying subtly underneath a pensive exterior. We stepped aside, out of the way of a group of women wearing green skirts and white blouses. Moving in unison as a row of twelve, they pushed brooms across a courtyard of marble, piously devoted to the upkeep of the golden shrine.

After leaving the temple, we walked the streets of Yangon, dodging the red blobs of chewed betel nut that had been spat every few inches by the locals. Chewing betel nut, considered somewhat of a national pastime, gave the chewer a nicotine-like buzz. Dev and I marvelled at how many of the skirt-clad people we passed had characteristic bright red grins. It seemed almost as though we were in a sea of vampires; nearly everyone we passed was chewing, spitting, and grinning a blood-red smile. We sat to rest on a bench in a central square, enjoying the shade of a weepy tree with low-hanging branches.

"We haven't really talked about it, but I think we are going to the same place," Dev said, approaching the topic delicately.

"To Lantau, right?" I replied.

"Yes, that's where I'm going. You are as well, I think."

"I am." I hesitated. "But how did you know?"

Dev glanced around us, smiling at an older man being helped down the street by a young boy who was firmly gripping the arm of his elder. "It was the way you looked at me, back in Puri, when I told you where I was going. You never brought it up again. So many others would have. I started to consider that my pilgrimage might not be quite as unique as I had thought." He looked at me, measuring my reaction to his observation.

"It is true. In Lantau, I hope to find help for …" I paused, suddenly feeling as though my intentions were too private to share.

"It's okay," Dev offered. "You don't have to explain. The journey is personal to all of us; I understand that. It's just, well, do you remember that bumblebee you rescued this morning?"

I nodded.

"I was thinking about what you did for that creature. And I was thinking about what we talked about in Puri, about sometimes we are the fish. And, well, I was thinking how far you've come and how many stops you've made and how many weeks it's taken you to make it this far and how much further you have to go …" His words came out in a tumble, and he finally stopped to catch his breath.

"If all goes well," I inserted, "I should be in Lantau in five days. By bus to Hong Kong, by boat to Lantau, and then a day of driving and hiking. I am almost there."

Dev smiled, seemingly impressed by the optimism of someone who'd been on the road for several weeks and was clearly weary. "Yes, five days. Well, that's what I wanted to talk to you about. You see, I want to do something for you. I want to buy you a plane ticket to Hong Kong. I know it's outside of your budget, you told me so yourself. It will diminish your journey by four days' length, and I see how tired you are from all of this travel, and, well, I want to do this for you. Money is something I have extra of and I want to … I … I want to be a fish to you and help you, like you helped the exhausted bee."

I looked at the misty eyes that had come over Dev and looked down at my hands, giving him the privacy grown men owe each other when one sheds tears in front of another.

I stood and walked a few paces away from the bench. Dev's offer was generous. I knew the tickets would cost him quite a bit. *Why do I feel so resistant to his offer? I feel unworthy of it and … I feel as though, if I had worked harder and had more money, it is I who would be helping him, not the other way around.*

I thought of my daughter then. I hadn't seen in her weeks, and with the remoteness of my travel stops, I had been unavailable to receive updates on her progress. I panicked suddenly, realizing she could be dead by the time I got home. I had been gone so long. *Accepting Dev's offer could mean I'll return home sooner, to my daughter, to my wife.*

Just then, from the corner of my eye, I saw again the older man being helped down the street by the younger one. He leaned into the youngster. The young man bore the weight of the older one. They progressed steadily onward. I watched as they disappeared around a corner.

I swallowed my pride and turned to Dev. "Your offer is generous, my friend. I am humbled to accept your assistance. I am grateful for it. Thank you for helping me." I bowed my head slightly in reverence, gratitude welling up in my heart for this helper.

He stood and slapped me hard on the back, jolting me out of a sombre moment, and grinned at me. "Well then, let's get to Hong Kong!"

Had I not accepted Dev's offer, I shudder now to think what might've happened, or more importantly, what might *not* have happened. Every opportunity, every step, every moment, every day, we are given chances and choices to swallow pride, to give ourselves in service to others as I had done with Dev and the bee. Of equal importance, we have chances to accept help from others. Had I declined Dev's offer, I would've been taking away from the blessing that would be his by giving to another, by giving to me. I would have, in essence, robbed him of an opportunity to give.

Giving of ourselves puts us in a position of humility to receive; our receiving spurs us to desire to give back more, and the cycle continues. We are all – human, beast, and bug – connected.

Ten

The Monk of Lantau

Be a lamp, or a lifeboat, or a ladder. Help someone's soul heal. Walk out of your house like a shepherd.

—Rumi

Zoe

"Yes, sir, I understand. ... It's fine, you can send her things here. ... Yes, that's the correct address. ... Thank you, I appreciate your help. ... I completely agree, it's unfortunate. ... Thank you again. ... Good day, sir. Goodbye."

I clicked off the call and set the phone down, sinking into the pillows of the worn couch in my flat. It no longer smelled like Elle, hadn't for a long while.

I considered the caller's message and inwardly grieved. This couldn't be good news. A box of her belongings was being sent to me from Stockholm, but where was the owner of those belongings, and what condition was she in now?

A mother's love can bear a great deal, but fear and angst over one's young daughter's whereabouts were things no mother should have to bear.

Matteo

Zoe's tale completed me in a way nothing else ever had. I wished I could have stayed in that moment forever, lingering amid the melody of her voice and the true, steady beat of my heart, recognizing the truth in her every word.

I look back on that day and marvel at how different my life might have been had I not taken up my instinct to pause at her table in the café and check in with her before leaving my shift. There are dividing points in our lives, before which and after which we categorize all things. Before Zoe, I had been a broke and happy artist, giving myself to help children express themselves on canvas. After Zoe, I was a gushing fountain, ready to drip, dribble, and soak any living thing I found that seemed to want for care and healing and the beautiful gifts of humanity.

I loved the person I became through Zoe's story. It gave me so much hope and reason and purpose in my existence. And it gave me love, a love so deep I felt sometimes as if it would consume me with bliss and gratitude. Because of Zoe's story, I am now a person deserving of the love I've found. The wealth of the fountain within me is more than enough to return to my beloved all that she gives me.

Nadine

Tehran had been healing for me. Not completely, but then again it had only been a few weeks. These things took time, and I knew I was on the right track.

The man I met on the train from Istanbul, Matthew, had started it all. His counsel on the power of forgiveness had been so unassuming, so pure in its offering, yet it had affected me more profoundly than anything else had. I sat down that night in the comfort of my rented room in Tehran and wrote down the name of my estranged husband, over and over again, until I had thoroughly recounted every ounce of pain he'd ever caused me, physical and emotional. Then, tearing the page in pieces, I burned each piece one by one in the flame of a candle lit on my bureau. I burned my fingers a couple of times, but the slight pain only served to singe the edges of the forgiveness I'd enveloped.

Certainly my heart still ached, but the weight of resentment had left me. I knew my marriage was over. And someday, I knew I would be open again to love. But I had a steel resolve in my heart to never be a victim to his abuse again and to pursue all avenues towards having my children returned to my safe and loving embrace.

And I had Matthew to thank for that.

I was left with a need to heal my heart completely, to return it to its full and unbroken state. As I spent my first few days in Tehran, exploring the markets and taking in the sights and smells and sounds of an achingly misunderstood city, I spoke to a man who was selling tea from a giant kettle balanced precariously on his frame. He told me of a way, of a place, of a path whereby I might find the healing I was looking for.

The next morning I packed my bags and headed east, no longer a despondent runaway, this time instead a determined and forgiving woman in search of a way to love again.

Dev

Our flight from Myanmar to Honk Kong was blessedly restful. After bumping along the waves on our sea voyage, Matthew and I sank gratefully into the luxurious accommodations of first class and ate and drank readily of all that was served to us. I was used to first-class seating, but I could tell Matthew was not. He held himself aloof for a bit, unsure and seemingly uncomfortable with being waited on. After a bit of this, I leaned over and whispered to him, my travel-weary friend, "Please, Matthew, enjoy my gift thoroughly. It is my joy for you to have it." After that, he visibly relaxed.

Matthew had been a puzzlement to me from the time I'd met him weeks ago in Puri. I had found him to be utterly gracious and kind, especially in dealing with the beggar who had robbed him. He had taught me a most invaluable method of healing my head from the aches that had plagued me for years. Selflessly he had listened for hours as I poured out my tale of woe, the story of how my business partner was robbing me and undermining me in every way. And just when I'd thought my friend could handle no more of my whining, he'd simply smiled at me and leaned forward to give his advice.

"Remember how the fishermen work, Dev," Matthew said. "Work like a fisherman. Be honest and true in your dealings with others. Covet no more than your day's need, and the universe will provide."

The puzzlement I had about Matthew was this: for all his wise words, for all the myriad ways he'd helped me personally, by his own tongue he was a mess of a human being. I could hardly believe him when he told me the story of his daughter and her accident, the guilt that clouded him because of it, the horrible ways he'd acted out against his wife and every person he'd met since. He told me how he'd slaved for his boss and his company, anxiously looking for ways to advance his career and earn a wage that would secure a more cushioned future for his family and how his temper was constantly unchecked and fuelled by greed and resentment. The way Matthew described himself was not the way I saw Matthew. To me, he was caring, good, patient, eager to help, self-sacrificing, and willing always to listen – really listen! – to my problems before offering the most cryptic, the most mystical words of advice. His advice, I'd found, was always spot on.

I closed my eyes in my airplane seat and carefully considered his latest advice regarding working as the fishermen do. It had helped me immensely to turn around the situation I now faced in business, and to look at my thieving partner from another angle. Of course, the situation would have to be dealt with, but realizing that I had plenty of success, money, and notoriety helped me take greed out of the equation. No longer was I worried as much about taking my partner to court for all he was worth. I would be content instead to extradite myself from our working relationship, with as much grace and forbearance as I could muster, for the sake of my sanity, not my pocket book.

I will never forget the day I learned my partner was stealing from the company. The anger I had had then was so palpable it must have been steaming from my ears. I stopped to buy a newspaper from a vendor in New Delhi, and he could not have escaped noticing my rage. He looked me in the eye and told me of the most wonderful place, a trek if you will, to a mountain where I could find all the answers I needed to solve my business problems. I had set out the next day towards Puri and the coast.

And now, several weeks later, having met Matthew and let his words soak into me and diffuse my anger, I was still intent on the destination the newspaper vendor had directed me towards. Maybe there I could find a way to forgive my partner for all of the ways in which he'd wronged me. That was the answer I still sought.

Nadine

I waited at the boat dock at the edge of the airport in Hong Kong, resigned to be patient as the time for my boat reservation drew closer. My excitement at finally reaching Lantau Island hammered in my chest with a ferocity that rivalled my anticipation at meeting my babies for the first time, the joy of a sunny spring morning in London, and the first sip of coffee in the morning, all rolled into one. I felt so close now, on the verge of finally making it to that magical destination on which I had pinned all my hopes for healing.

Dev

Groggy from our flight, Matthew and I approached the boat dock at the edge of the airport in Hong Kong. I wrestled within myself to be patient and calm, but my heart was thudding with excitement at the thought of suddenly being so close to Lantau Island. Finally, we were nearly there.

From the corner of my eye, I saw a woman waving frantically at me. She was tall and stately in blue western-style boots, her hair was drawn away from her face. The milk-white skin of her neck and arms was dazzlingly beautiful. From where he was walking beside me, I heard Matthew exclaim, "Nadine! Oh, wow! How can this be? How are you possibly here? I thought you were in—"

"Tehran?" The woman smiled at us and spoke directly to Matthew.

Ah, that's why she was waving. She knows Matthew somehow.

The two hugged and greeted each other like dear old friends, and for a moment I felt like an outsider.

"Nadine, this is my good friend Dev. Dev, this is Nadine, from London. I met her on my journey out of Istanbul." Matthew was grinning from ear to ear, obviously happy to be surrounded by friends in a world so far from home.

We talked as we waited for the boat and marvelled that, by some miracle, we were all en route to Lantau Island, to the top of a hill, to a place where a Buddha sat. We were going there for different reasons, though we didn't share those reasons openly then.

I remember thinking it was a very, very strange coincidence. But then again, according to Matthew, there were no coincidences.

Our boat ride was calm, and the early morning light was lovely. As we approached Lantau Island, we each remarked on the peace and tranquillity the island exuded, with its green banks appearing magically from behind a curtain of mist.

I stole a glance at my companions and noted with a smile that they were quietly taking in our surroundings.

Nadine

What amazing luck to have found Matthew again. Somehow it seemed fitting that we were together, concluding the journey that had introduced us to each other. Our boat docked and we boarded a bus that began a steady ascent up a primitive road riddled with potholes, winding, winding, winding up the sides of the dense green hills before us. I stole a glance at my companions; each was lost in his own thoughts.

Knowing what I had come to see for myself about Matthew – how congenial and friendly, wise and helpful he is – it came as no surprise that he'd made another friend along his journey. Dev was striking with his turban and pressed clothes, looking so nicely put together for a man who had by his own account been travelling through India and Myanmar to get here. I felt frumpy and sweaty in my travelling clothes, but he looked as cool and collected as could be.

Through the mist we first saw the peak of the hill we were destined for. It emerged slowly, as if nature were pulling aside the curtains for us at slow speed for dramatic effect. I sucked in my breath, creating a soft whistle through my teeth. Matthew and Dev looked at me, and we were caught in a moment of wide-eyed anticipation and joy. We were here. We had made it to Lantau, to the destination we each sought for different reasons.

Only one question remained. What were we supposed to do next?

Dev

As we disembarked from the rickety bus, the bronze statue of the Buddha rose before us, in a reverent and holy display of awesomeness. Never before had I seen a Buddha so tall, so stately, so ... present.

Glancing at Matthew, I sensed he was as awestruck as I was.

Together, the three of us ascended the steps leading to the base of the statue. Quietly, willing our feet to hush in supreme respect, we walked the circumference of the Buddha, who was in seated pose, his right hand raised as a signal of removing affliction and his left hand laid in his lap in a gesture of giving *dhana*. We leisurely completed our loop, taking in the magic of the moment and relishing our collective sense of having arrived, finally, at our destination.

I was puzzled though. What I had been told to look for was not here, not the way the newspaper vendor had described it. Looking around me, I noted there were only a few people there, and a sombre-looking docent standing watch over the area. Matthew stepped forward to speak to the docent. Nadine and I held back, watching.

Momentarily, Matthew returned to us and softly said, "What we seek is not here; it's down the hill a way." He gestured to a direction below the Buddha, below the stairs, somewhere in the trees. We followed his lead.

Moving more quickly now, we traipsed down the steps and down a small dirt path half-obscured by an overgrowth of trees. We were drawn by an undeniably strong, invisible attraction. And soon, after several minutes of walking, we arrived at a hut with a thatched roof made of stripped branches.

My heart was pounding, and I felt a sense of being on hallowed ground. Matthew hung back, taking in our surroundings and measuring the hut with his eyes, as if unsure of what he might find if he stepped closer. Nadine and I looked at each other over his head. As our eyes met, we silently agreed on our course of action. Stepping behind Matthew, we gently nudged him forward towards the hut.

"Go in, Matthew. See if he is there. You should be the first to meet the healer," I said.

"Yes, Matthew, we will wait for you here. Please, it should be you first, for all you've done for us," Nadine added.

Matthew took a step towards the hut and walked slowly around the side to the door on the front, away from our ability to see him entering. Through the back window facing us, we could see him moving into the hut. He paced back and forth in front of the window, looking more and more confused with each pass.

After several moments, he came back out and said plainly, "It's empty. There's no one there."

"Are you sure, Matthew? Take another look!" Nadine said.

Matthew shrugged and walked back inside. We saw him pass in front of the window and stand still, with his back towards us. Just then, the sun came out from behind the cloud that had been masking it all day. A ray shone into the hut through a gap in the thatching, illuminating Matthew in a glow of heavenly light. He stood perfectly still, basking in the single, stray ray of light.

The forest around us became still and perfectly silent. I held my breath and watched, transfixed by the magic of what was happening, wondering if I was seeing it clearly. It looked to me, and to this day I'll swear by it, that a figure joined him, the figure of a man of great age. They were side by side and their arms were around each other, heads bent together in soundless discussion. And then, in an instant, the light was gone and Matthew was standing alone.

Nadine

I cannot say how it happened, only that it did, and I was there to bear witness, along with Dev. We both saw the same thing. Now, years later, I cannot deny the picture of it that still registers as clear as day in my memory.

When Matthew emerged from the hut, he was a changed man. He moved with a grace that made me do a double-take and look down at his feet to be sure they were in contact with the ground. He glided as he walked; he hovered as if on a thin cloud that kept him from touching earth. And his skin. Oh, his skin was the most amazing thing. It was like light itself, shimmering and translucent, glittering and glinting in the sun like a veil of diamonds.

He walked towards us slowly, emanating a great peace. Coming close to where Dev and I stood, he laid a hand on each of our arms and circled us together with his touch. His smile was heavenly, like a warm hug on a cold night, and invoked such surpassing peace that his whole being was like the incarnation of peace itself.

As he touched me, I understood all. I knew a healing in my heart that crept upon me with such gentleness, such knowing, that I held my breath and prayed it would soak so deeply inside me that I'd never lose it.

From that moment, I was changed.

I looked over at Dev and saw on his face the same awe and joy that I felt. I reached for his hand.

Matthew walked ahead of us, and we began our return journeys to our respective homes.

As we walked, I looked up at Dev. I whispered in his ear something about writing names on paper, forgiving in one's heart, letting go in order to find much more than one ever had before. In his eyes, I saw the reflection of a soul I would cherish forever. For a split second, I thought I saw him grasping my hand and chasing children across a green lawn. And those children looked ever so much like my own.

Epilogue

When angels visit us, we do not hear the rustle of wings,
nor feel the feathery touch of the breast of a dove; but we
know their presence by the love they create in our hearts.

—Mary Baker Eddy

Zoe

The sound of a knock at the door made me jump. I went to answer it, thinking it was too soon for a deliveryman to have feasibly been able to deliver Elle's things from Stockholm. As I pulled open the door, I was greeted with the warm and cheery smile of a new friend who felt like an old friend.

"Zoe! So good to see you! I'm sorry to surprise you like this!" Matteo stepped into the big hug I offered him, and we embraced.

"Come in! Please, come in!" I was excited to see Matteo, but it was such a surprise. *How did he even know where I lived?*

Matteo entered and followed me as I led him to the kitchen and began heating water for tea.

"Oh, um, Zoe ... tea sounds so good right now, I could really use a cup, but actually, I can't stay long ..." Matteo's tone was distant and mysterious. I set down the kettle to turn and look at him.

"You just got here! Already you have to go? I don't understand."

"Um, well, actually, there's something I need to show you. I was hoping you could come with me to see it?" Matteo extended his hand as if to invite me to grasp it and follow him.

"Well, that's pretty mysterious of you, Matteo, but give me a minute and I'll go grab my coat." I smiled warmly at him.

We walked briskly down the street, Matteo and I. All of my questions about where we were going and what we were doing went unanswered. He wouldn't divulge a thing as he pulled me along, sidestepping people and bikes and benches and shops and parked cars until finally we stopped.

I looked around me. It was a park, the one I used to take Elle to when she was young.

"Matteo, I don't understand. You brought me to a park? But why?" I was curious but also growing a little annoyed to have been pulled out into the cold on this dreary day. I would much rather have been tucked in with a nice cup of tea in my comfortable kitchen.

"Over there," Matteo said, pointing in the direction of the centre of the park. "Look over there."

I followed his outstretched fingers and nearly fainted on the spot. Matteo's grip held me upright and supported me as we walked, arms linked, towards the grassy expanse at the park's centre.

My Elle stood in the middle of a ring of easels. Before each easel stood a child, maybe 5 or 6 or 7 years old. Each child held a brush in one hand and a palette of colour in the other. Each easel was quickly becoming a masterpiece of design, texture, and contour.

"Careful now. Don't rush to be finished. Let your heart guide you towards that moment when your piece is complete," said Elle, attentively hovering over a small boy with a mischievous grin spread across his face.

She looked up, and for the first time in nearly a year, our eyes met. Mine and hers. I steadied my gaze, searching her face for signs of what her reaction might be to seeing me there, ready to dodge and run from a scowl and equally ready to race into her embrace if her eyes invited me to.

"Mum!" Elle called to me, arms outstretched, moving quickly in my direction.

I held her and we rocked together, hugging and laughing and crying all at once.

"How? Why? I … I don't understand!" I said to Elle, my voice muffled by her hair, and her shoulder covering my mouth. I couldn't let her go. I wouldn't let her go. I'd missed her so much.

We broke apart at the touch of Matteo on each of our shoulders.

"Elle, why don't you take a walk with your mum? I can finish up here." His voice was soft and held a note of tenderness and intimacy. It hadn't escaped my notice. I looked quickly back and forth from Elle to Matteo and back to Elle.

Elle grabbed my hand and pulled at me, and we began walking.

"Mum," Elle started, "I can't begin to tell you how sorry I am for all I put you through …"

We must've walked and talked for hours as the daylight faded, about her life in Stockholm and the way her internship ended, how abruptly she had left the law firm without even returning to her desk to clean it out. Her boss had called me to say he was returning her things to her. She told me about the despair she felt at thinking of spending her whole life working in an office, in a profession that seemed heartless and cruel at times, one that didn't allow her an opportunity to give back and share and create and spread joy to others.

"And then, Mum, I walked into that café. You know, the one by the waterfront. You were there once, waiting for me. And Matteo found me. He brought me tea and we started talking and, Mum, he told me the most amazing story." Elle's words came out in a rush, like the waves of water long pent up behind a dam, now released.

"Mum," she continued, "we're getting married, Matteo and I. We started an art school, right here in London, for underprivileged kids. Our classes are free and all the materials are supplied. I can't tell you how amazing it is to be surrounded by the love these little hands create every day. These kids are finding healing and compassion through creating and painting and imagining ..." I hugged her so hard then, crushing her thin frame in my embrace, my heart overflowing with love for the return of my daughter to me.

"But sweetheart, you're saying you've been in London for a while now? Why didn't you ... I didn't even know!" The realisation that months of wondering where she was and how she fared were all a waste, given that she had been right here and so close to me the whole time, was almost too much to bear.

"I couldn't come to you right away, Mum. I had so much stuff to work through and deal with, and the timing wasn't right. And then I met a man, as if by coincidence. The next day, he and I and Matteo had lunch. He told me that he'd been looking for me for quite some time. He's funding our entire school, no questions asked! Whatever we need! It was like we'd known each other forever." She stopped talking and looked at me. Her eyes grew wide and tears began to fall, trickling delicately down her beautiful face.

"Who is the man, Elle?" My voice quieted as I asked my question. A thudding in my chest told me I already knew the answer.

"His name is Dev, Mum, and he gave me these." She held out a packet of papers as thick as a dictionary, all different colours and textures, filled with words in languages I couldn't even decipher.

"But what are these?" I asked.

"They're letters, Mum – letters people wrote to Daddy, thanking him for everything he had done for them, how he changed their lives, how much hope and joy he'd given them. I read them all, and that's when I told Matteo it was time for me to see you again. I know who Dad was, Mum. I know now how I healed from wounds that should have killed me. It was Dad. I remember now. His hands, his love, his care … He came to me in my hospital room, his skin shimmering like diamonds, and he surrounded me with his energy and his love for me, and I woke up the next day from my coma and told the first nurse I saw that I was ready to come home."

I was sobbing uncontrollably. This, all this and more, made his life worth living. All he went through to become the man, the person, the amazing person he became, was worth it. Our daughter had realised her potential, turned a corner, and met her destiny head on with all the strength and grace and beauty her dad and I had always dreamed of for her. I wished he could see it. Somehow, I knew he did.

We looked up at the sky, me and my beautiful, whole, shimmering daughter, and watched as a star streaked across it. I knew then that Elle's dad was watching, smiling at her, and loving us both from up above.

Author's Note

The Tian Tan Buddha, or the Big Buddha, is 112 feet tall, weighs 250 tons, and is made of bronze. The statue is located near Po Lin Monastery on Lantau Island in Hong Kong. A popular tourist attraction, it is a major centre of Buddhism in Hong Kong. More than that though, the statue symbolizes the harmonious relationship between man and nature, people and religion.

The site where the Buddha sits is somewhat mysterious in itself. No one is exactly sure why this site was chosen. Though the statue wasn't completed until 1993, there were many hundreds of years prior to that when it is said a smaller version of the Buddha sat in the same place, perhaps brought there on foot by a healer who had travelled many miles.

The Author

Mann was born in London in 1979.

Although he is widely recognised for his entrepreneurial flair, his contributions to society, culture, and philanthropy run much deeper and stem from a personal philosophy to live a compassionate and grateful life.

In his desire to help others, he has attained the privilege status of a Reiki Master Teacher. He uses this art to heal individuals of their physical, emotional and mental imbalances through the power of positive energy.

Mann himself went through a lengthy period of darkness in his personal life until, as if by accident, he stumbled upon a path of self-realisation, culminating in inner peace.

The Monk of Lantau is Mann's gift to those who are still searching for this peace. It is an inspirational fiction work that honours the journey our lives take through self-discovery to attain an existence steeped in balance, compassion, forgiveness, and enlightenment.

Lightning Source UK Ltd.
Milton Keynes UK
UKOW02f2332200815

257287UK00001B/9/P